In the Heart of a Valentine Book One

By

Stephanie Nicole Norris

Acknowledgments

Wow, it's been a been a journey writing these stories from my heart, and I want to take a moment to acknowledge a few of you who have been instrumental with helping me through this process.

Special thanks first and foremost to my readers. You guys are amazing, and I love each and every one of you. To my illustrator Amy Q. To be able to take my vision and bring it to my cover is amazing, and I am in awe of you! To my editor Shonell Bacon, your critique is so influential and priceless to me! Thank you for having my back and being a part of my team!

To my literary partner in crime Deidra D. S. Green, you have so many roles I can't name them all. LOL. Thank you for having my back and being my sounding board when I'm crazy and trying to write 50-thousand books at one time. ;)

To Travis Cure, thank you for allowing me to use your

image to bring Hunter Valentine to life! I appreciate you and wish you much success in all your endeavors.

Last but certainly not least, my family and friends. My son Noah, my husband Patrick, my mother Jessica. You guys are my squad, and I love you for life and hereafter!

This gift I have wouldn't be possible without my Lord and Savior manifesting it within me. Thank you, God, for everything. Your daughter, Steph.

Dedication

To all of you who continue to read my stories. If you haven't already I hope you find your happily ever after.

Chapter One

"*I* know, Mom, I'm sorry. It was late when I got in."

Camilla Augustina rubbed her eyes and tossed the duvet off as she rolled to her side. Laying her iPhone on the pillow, Camilla hit the speaker button and struggled to pull her now sweaty nightgown over her head. When she'd laid down for rest, there was a chill inside her new apartment, but now it was just plain old hot.

"You know I worry if you don't call when you say you will," Sharon Augustina fussed.

"If I had actually called after I got settled, you would've thought something was wrong because of the late-night hour," Camilla replied.

Sharon let out a soft sigh. "Why didn't you let your father ride up with you? Then at least I would've gotten some sleep last night."

"No, you wouldn't. I know you too well, Mom. You'd

have just switched from worrying about one of us to both of us."

Sharon pursed her lips. "But your father would've called. Anyway, I won't bother you too much about it. I know you have a new job to freshen up and go to."

There was a smile in Sharon's soft graceful tone. Sharon was so proud of her child for landing the anchor position at WTZB in Chicago that she squealed with delight when they both found out. It was bittersweet, since for all of Camilla's thirty-eight years, she'd lived in her hometown of Miami. Going from sunny skies, humid weather, and beach life to the windy city of Chicago was a big change that Camilla wasn't sure she would like yet. Regardless, Camilla would find a way. WTZB had picked her over one hundred and fifty candidates they inter- viewed from all over for the position. However, Camilla's master's degree in journalism along with her seven-year position as an anchor at News 12 in the sunshine state, made her the top pick. Not to mention her pleasurable personality, expanded answers, and ability to catch on quickly during the rigorous three-tier interview which sealed the deal.

Camilla glanced at the time on her phone. 5 a.m.

"Thank you. As you can see, Mother, I made it to Chicago safe and sound. It's a great thing that I moved my stuff a few weeks in advance so all I had to do was grab a rental and GPS my way to my apartment."

"Mmhmm, if not, then I definitely would've made your father fly up with you. Did the rental company give you any hassle?"

"No, they had my reservation and the car waiting for me, how about that, huh?"

Sharon recognized her child's mocking tone. "One day you'll understand why I put up so much fuss when you have your own kids."

The thought of kids was horrifying to Camilla. In Camilla's young adult years, she'd worked as a daycare teacher while getting her degree. There were times when spending time with the children was a delight, but then there were those children who screamed when their parents left—blood-curdling screams as if they had been maimed. Camilla could never quite get them settled after that, and the day would be a blizzard of out of control activity. The experience made Camilla think twice about having kids of her own. And with the shortage of loyal men in the world, she'd decided not to go down that road at all.

"I highly doubt that," Camilla responded. "But you're right, I need to get ready for work."

"Okay, I'll be looking to catch you on the news this morning, dear."

"Actually, today may be preliminary, so I could very well start in front of the camera tomorrow."

"I understand. I'll look anyway."

Camilla snickered. "Okay, Mom, talk to you later."

"I love you, dear."

"I love you, too."

Camilla ended the call and rolled to the other side of her bed and stretched. After lingering a minute or two longer, she pulled herself from the comfort of her sheets then trudged to the bathroom and flipped on the lights. As the brightness flooded the room, Camilla squinted, waiting for her eyes to adjust.

"We here at WTZB want to thank you for watching. Have a Happy Valentine's Day," Camilla auditioned to herself. A satisfied smile cruised across her face, spreading her full lips into a beaming grin. The soft brown eyes that looked back at her held excitement, and the butterflies in her stomach tussled as she thought about the day ahead of her.

It had taken Camilla an hour and a half to get ready. Which was good timing in her opinion. Even though she prepared last night by showering and having her pinstripe suit and briefcase ready, the sweaty night she'd endured prompted her to take another shower. She could've easily been ready in thirty minutes, but Camilla took extra care of her appearance, adding a layer of foundation that heightened her sienna skin and moisturizer to her hair that gave it a light bounce, just in case they did decide to throw her on camera.

Grabbing her case and coffee, Camilla checked her watch and decided there was enough time for her to grab breakfast from the restaurant downstairs. She opened the door and stepped into the hallway then paused as three women dressed in skimpy dresses and high heel shoes exited the only other apartment on the floor.

The last one turned back and crooned, "We'll be looking for your call later, so don't keep us waiting…"

"Did I promise to call you," a deep voice thundered.

The sound of the baritone vocals drummed down Camilla's skin, causing her to take a step back into her apartment and push the door closed quickly. With it slightly ajar, Camilla leaned against the wooden frame and continued to listen as the two made their parting comments.

"As if you won't." The tall, limber woman laughed, light and carefree.

"I've got a busy day ahead of me, sweetheart. I can't afford such luxuries if I didn't."

The woman laughed again. "You could afford anything you want," she said. "Including me."

Camilla frowned and pushed her lips out. *You can afford me?* "This girl must have daddy issues," she whispered. Their voices paused for such a long time that Camilla almost stuck her head out the door. But when the woman sauntered past Camilla's entryway, Camilla closed it even further, making sure not to make so much as a peep.

It wasn't every day that Camilla snooped on her next-door neighbors. In fact, Camilla's neighbors in Florida were Puerto Rican, and she could hardly understand what they said, most of the time anyway. She wondered if the women were high-priced prostitutes that helped her mystery neighbor get his fix for the night. Camilla rolled her eyes and waited for the three women to get on the elevator.

When she heard a ding, Camilla rested assured that she wouldn't run into them. It was then that she took her leave, dashing out of the door and locking it quickly, then taking a fast-paced strut to the elevator. As she waited, Camilla couldn't help but wonder what the man behind the voice looked like. She thought of Idris Elba and Lance Gross, then smirked.

"What do you care?" she whispered. *Leave your mystery*

man just that. A mystery. But Camilla knew why she cared, and it behooved her to not even meet the mystery man though she was currently salivating over his voice. "Wait a minute," Camilla said. She tracked back to the last thought. Since when did he become *your* mystery man? Camilla shook her head. "I'm trippin' already. I thought you'd be in Chicago a little longer before you started to lose it," she joked. "And I'm standing here talking to myself," she mumbled. "Greaaat."

The elevator dinged then the door opened, and Camilla shuffled quickly inside. When the metal doors closed, she breathed, letting out an exasperated breath like she'd been holding it the entire time she stood waiting to get inside the safety of the tin can. Camilla pulled her wrist up and glanced at her watch. She hadn't wasted too much time snooping on her neighbor so that was a good thing.

The elevator reached the bottom floor in record time, with no stops between. Camilla was delighted by that. She knew the high-rise building was home to famous faces. Football, basketball, and even a few hockey players lived in the building, along with a politician or two. Businessmen and women from Chicago also called The Regency their home. It was one of the reasons Camilla chose the location. Being among them assured that security in the building was tighter than Fort Knox. That, and it wouldn't be a bad thing to be a resident in a place that could possibly grant her a story.

Camilla's heels click-clacked against the marble floor as she found her way inside Benjamin's Breakfast Hut.

"Good morning," a hostess chimed as she entered.

"Good morning," Camilla replied. She glanced around

the bistro, noting the bustling activity. "It seems you have a full house."

The hostess looked around as if she hadn't notice.

"I have a special spot just for you," the hostess sang.

Camilla perked. "I'm following," she sang back.

The hostess put on a bright smile. "Right this way." She turned with a sharp twist and meandered easily through the restaurant.

A few busboys passed them as they headed for a table to the far right of the eatery. "Excuse me," one said as he scurried around Camilla, wiping a hand on the neatly folded apron tied around his waist.

"How's this," the hostess said, stopping at a small table.

"You did have the perfect spot," Camilla said, staring out the window to the hustling Chicagoans who strolled through the downtown streets. "Nice and tidy, too," she continued taking a seat at the short table.

"Yeah, we're always crowded this early. Are you new to The Regency?"

Camilla smiled. "Yes, I am."

The hostess' eyes popped. "In that case, let me be one of the first to welcome you to Benjamin's Breakfast Hut. I'm Alicia, it's nice to meet you."

"Camilla," Camilla said, offering her a handshake.

"That's a pretty name," Alicia beamed.

"Thank you."

"Camilla, your server will be with you in just a second."

"Thank you again," Camilla responded. She set her briefcase down and pulled out her cell phone. Camilla could sit for thirty minutes before she made her way to work. The beauty of being on the staff at WTZB was that it was within walking distance of The Regency, which was another plus when Camilla decided to rent a space in the luxury towers. It had only cost her a small fortune to lease the mini penthouse suite, but it was well worth the security and convenience.

She strolled through her missed calls. Two of them were from her friend Corinne Thomas whom Camilla had worked with for five of her seven years at News 12 before Corinne left the studio to become a stewardess. Camilla was also supposed to call Corinne for safe check-in as well. The other five missed calls were from Stephen her ex-boyfriend, the last person Camilla wanted to talk to.

After being engaged to Stephen for three years, Stephen suddenly decided marriage wasn't for him. He called it off the minute Camilla began bridal shopping. Six months later, Stephen was back, begging for a chance to show Camilla he'd changed. For three months, Camilla let him fester and beg like the dog he was, but she eventually took him back. Another two years of her life later and Stephen was doing it again, calling off the wedding. Camilla had had enough, letting Stephen know there would never be another chance for them. That was eight months ago and now he was back again, ringing up her phone, probably wondering why there was a for sale sign in her yard.

Camilla skipped right over his number and hit send on Corinne's. "Pony" by Ginuwine cruised through the receiver, and Camilla frowned.

"I was just getting ready to put an ABP out on you," Corinne answered.

"Before we can move any further with this conversation, I need to know why Ginuwine is singing to me when I'm calling you. Is that seriously one of those ring back tones?"

Corinne cleared her throat. "Oh, so you didn't have Missy Elliot singing when someone called you?"

Camilla's lips thinned out. "Yeah, like ten years ago."

"Whatever."

Camilla laughed in whispered tones. "What happens when your boss calls and 'Pony' plays in his ear?" Camilla continued to laugh.

"I like how you just flipped this whole conversation around to me," Corinne said. "I suppose you're safe." Corinne's voice was stern, and Camilla knew she'd upset her.

"Aww, okay, I'm sorry. There's nothing wrong with your ring back tone," Camilla lied. She dropped her head in her hand and shook it slightly. "I'm okay. Thank you for calling to check on me."

"I told you I would, didn't I?"

"Yeah, you did. And I wish we could've come up on the weekend together."

"Ooh, that would've been nice. Then I could get all up in your Chicago business."

Camilla chuckled. "I don't have any Chicago business. Yet, anyway—"

"*Excuse* me…"

The timbre of his voice not only sent a shrill of heat cascading over Camilla's body, but it also caught her by surprise and threw her off balance. Bringing her eyes up to the mystery man himself, Camilla's heart skipped a beat as her sight took in the magnificence of his stature. Black suit pants laced around his powerful thighs and what Camilla knew was probably a taut ass. A leather Christian Dior belt buckle aligned through the loopholes of his pants, holding a pristine shine.

The maroon long sleeve button-down shirt stretched up the barrier of his grandiose wall of muscle and waved slightly over the pecs in his chest. With his collar flipped down and the first two buttons undone, his unblemished coffee brown skin was displayed. Camilla swallowed so hard she could've ingested her tongue. Her heart binged in her chest, and Camilla had a hard time trying to recover.

As if the palpitations weren't bad enough, Camilla's gaze locked with her mystery man, and immediately, she felt pulled toward him. With piercing dark brown eyes, he held her stare just as his tongue cruised across his lips to wet his mouth.

"I don't mean to interrupt you, but, there's nowhere else to sit while I have my breakfast, so I was hoping you'd have mercy on me and allow me to dine with you."

"Corinne," Camilla said, speaking into the phone, "I'm going to call you back."

Chapter Two

*C*amilla quickly scanned the restaurant. He was right, there was nowhere to sit, and she already knew that. He waited patiently for her to respond, taking a long accessing eye over the details of her face.

"Sure," she eased out, still slightly flustered.

"I'm Hunter Valentine, by the way, and you are?"

"Camilla."

Hunter reached out for a handshake.

"Good morning, Camilla. That's a beautiful name."

For some reason, when he'd complimented her name, it felt different than when the hostess had. It cruised through her body with a heated sting and settled right in her center. Camilla blushed, accepting his hand. The spark that tinged her fingers, looped around her skin, and spread throughout her loins.

Oh God, Camilla thought. What the hell was happening?

"Thank you, please, have a seat," she ushered.

Hunter's massive frame and elongated height were so domineering that when he sat, his legs stretched to Camilla's side of the table, touching her knee with a stimulating brush. Camilla's mouth parted, and a breath escaped her. And as if Camilla knew she'd start drooling at any moment, she shut her lips and easily crossed her legs to keep the exhilarating tingle from coursing down her spine in a constant vibration.

The server appeared in that instant, and he couldn't have come at a better time.

"Can I have a glass of water, please?" Camilla asked, keeping her voice steady and neutral. Why her nerves were on edge was a mystery that eluded her every second Hunter sat staring at her mouth. Which had only been a few but felt like a million.

"Yes, ma'am. I'm Ralph by the way. Would you like anything else or just water?"

"You know what, Ralph? A cup of cappuccino will be fine."

"Instead of water?"

"Yes, thank you."

"Okay, and you, sir?"

Camilla tried to force herself from taking her attention to Hunter's luscious lips, but looking at his penetrating observation, smooth brown skin, and striking features wasn't any better. Slowly, she took in a deep breath as Hunter spoke to their server. Camilla remembered his voice as if he'd whispered in her ear, and Camilla's drums had recorded a sonogram of the tone.

"I'll be right back," the server said, disappearing to fulfill their order.

"So, Camilla," Hunter began, "are you new around here?"

Camilla smirked. "Do I appear new to you, Hunter?"

Hunter smiled, a tantalizing smirk. "A woman who answers a question with a question," he mused. "Interesting…"

Camilla shifted slightly. "What's so interesting about that?"

Hunter shrugged his widespread shoulders. "If a person answers a question with a question, they usually have something to hide."

Camilla arched a brow. "Usually, huh, and what are you, a therapist?"

A deep, devouring laugh escaped him. "Nah, I wouldn't say that."

"Well what would you say?"

"I'd say you don't like talking about yourself to strangers and that's why you're avoiding my question. Never mind that it's a simple one. I wonder how you'd clam up if I asked you a personal one."

Another tingle sailed around Camilla's skin, and she licked her lips.

"Yes," Camilla reverted. "I've lived in this building all of twenty-four hours initially."

"Initially?"

"To be precise, I moved in two weeks ago. But I've just only made my debut late last night."

Hunter was intrigued. Who was this clandestine woman

flying into town in the middle of the night just to throw his equilibrium off early this morning. He had no plans to stop and have breakfast until he spotted her while he was walking past the bistro headed for the exit.

"Your name rings familiar," Camilla said, interrupting his thoughts.

A prevalent grin tapered across his face.

"By that award-winning smile, I'd say there's a reason for that," Camilla continued.

"I own VFC Energy," he plainly stated.

Camilla's eyes bucked. "The Fortune 500 company?"

Hunter's grin returned. "Yes."

"Hunter Valentine…" Camilla said at the awe-inspiring revelation.

Camilla had had the chance of reporting on Hunter twice in her anchor position at News 12. It was when he made headlines for beginning his green energy initiatives three years ago. The news topped CNN for almost a week, which was a rarity.

"Congratulations," Camilla said.

At the arch of Hunter's brow, Camilla elaborated. "On all of your success. Your parents must be really proud." She smiled, and Hunter's gaze dropped to her lips.

"Indeed, they are," he said. "Camilla…" his deep voice strummed when he spoke her name, causing Camilla to shiver involuntarily, "I wish I had the pleasure of knowing who you are. Tell me a little bit about yourself."

Camilla's serenaded laugh teetered on the edge of nervousness and a sensuality that sent a jolting buzz crawling down Hunter's skin. If he could bottle the sound to use at a time when he was perhaps having a bad day, it would definitely lighten his mood.

"I'm afraid I'm not as interesting as you," Camilla said.

"I don't believe that for a second."

When Camilla laughed again, it was low with a captivating jingle. The tone sent another thrill of exuberant energy slipping over his skin, making Hunter more anxious to know her background.

The server appeared with Camilla's cappuccino and Hunter's coffee. When the waiter sat a plate down bearing a stuffed omelet sidled with strawberries, blueberries, and diced oranges, Camilla peered up at him.

"I didn't order this."

"I did," Hunter's hypnotic voice grooved.

Camilla's eyes fluttered over to him, and she sat back against her seat. The memory of Hunter ordering escaped her, probably since Camilla was too busy staring at his mouth instead of listening to his words.

"Oh," was all she said.

"Is there anything else I can do for either of you?"

"I'm fine," Camilla said.

"That goes for the both of us," Hunter added.

"Okay, I'll be back in a minute to check on you two."

They both nodded as the waiter dashed off.

"I almost sent your dish back to the kitchen." Camilla laughed that nervous sultry laugh again, and Hunter's lips spread easily across his perfect face.

"Our dish," he retorted.

"Hmm?"

"I had this made for us to share," he added.

Camilla's mouth parted for a response, but it evaded her for longer than she liked. "I don't know you, Hunter, what makes you think I'd share your food? That's kind of personal, don't you think?"

"True, but I was hoping by the end of this conversation, we would be personally acquainted."

Camilla's brows rose. "How exactly do you propose that would happen?"

Hunter retrieved the butter knife from the wrapped napkin and added a fork to his massive hand. With a slow and even pace, he cut into the omelet and steam rose from the hot dish as bell peppers, cheese, meat, and other vegetables oozed out of it. Scooping the portion up on his utensil, Hunter held the fork just below her mouth then leaned in and blew over the toasty piece, causing the heat from the omelet to caress the top of her lips along with his cinnamon-scented breath.

The move was so erotically entangled that Camilla's heart was now slamming against her chest, and her nerves were set to dive off a cliff. When she spoke, Camilla didn't know who the voice belonged to from the thick sultry concoction of it.

Keeping her eyes on Hunter, Camilla said, "How do you even know I like my omelet mixed with these ingredients? If you really wanted to split this dish, you would've ordered a cheese omelet to be on the safe side."

Hunter's grin was laced with a mischief rue. "Maybe because somehow I know you're the kind of woman who likes to spice things up. In any case, there's nothing plain about you..."

Hunter's gaze roamed the contours of Camilla's face and his long thick lashes hovered above the brimming depth of his eyes. Thoroughly heated now, Camilla almost panted and didn't recognize herself as she leaned forward, opened her mouth, and settled her tongue between the utensil and the food. With a succulent pull, Camilla moaned and closed her eyes as she drew the warm entree off the fork shortly followed by a swiping of her tongue.

When Camilla reopened her eyes, Hunter's brown orbs held a stark darkness that ruffled her feathers and dropped a tingling burn over her flesh.

"My turn," Camilla said. She reached for the fork when Hunter spoke up.

"Nah… hands," he said.

Camilla arched a brow and sat the fork down on the table. With her fingers, she speared off a piece of omelet, the heat, seeping into her fingers. She held the food midways before sending a light blow of her own over the top. Unhurriedly, Camilla lifted the omelet to his lips, and in turn, Hunter covered her fingers with his mouth. The heated wetness of his aperture sent an effusion crawling up Camilla's skin that erected her nipples and caused her vagina to thump like a ricocheting headboard.

She thought, *oh my God*, but it came out like a whimpering pant. What the hell was happening? Why was she acting so out of character? Camilla didn't know Hunter from day or night. This was ridiculous. All those thoughts ran through Camilla, but her actions negated them. Instead of pulling back and snapping out of it like her mind screamed, she held, nice and steady, as Hunter took joy in licking and sucking each individual finger even the ones that held no flavor whatsoever. As she watched, Camilla followed the flip of his tongue, and enjoyed the delicate but hungry way he savored her flesh. Her heart was tap dancing now, and a stabilizing zing coated Camilla completely. When she felt herself moving in to meet his hungry mouth with hers an internal alarm triggered, warning her that she was not this person.

Finally jolting from her trance, Camilla cleared her throat and eased her hand back. She didn't know what to say, but she glanced at her time and realized she'd been having too much fun because the half an hour had gotten away from her.

Camilla cleared her throat again. "How was it?" she asked. "Better than my scoop?" A small smile cornered her mouth.

"Best damn fingers I've ever had," he said.

A sultry guffaw slipped from Camilla as she tossed her head back and laughed. Hunter smiled in return and combed his gaze over the lean stretch of her neck, wanting to move his mouth there next.

The waiter returned to their table. "Would you like a refill of your cappuccino," he asked Camilla.

Camilla checked her watch again. "Ah, sure, but let me have it in a to-go cup, please."

"Yes, ma'am."

"Are you in a hurry?" Hunter asked, not ready for this time with her to end.

"First day on the job," Camilla smiled brightly. "You know, since it's my first day as an official Chicagoan."

Hunter smiled. "You're not an official Chicagoan until you've met the president."

Camilla's eyes widened. "As in President Barak Obama?"

"Of course, that's my president." Camilla laughed haughtily. "Would you like to meet him?"

Camilla's smile stretched across her face. The server reappeared with her cappuccino.

"Will this be one check or two," the server asked.

Hunter and Camilla spoke at the same time, "Same check."

Camilla and Hunter eyed each other.

"Interesting…" Hunter said.

"Why's that?" Camilla retorted. "It's not every day I go around paying for a stranger's check."

"No," Hunter's deep voice stroked her, "just me..."

Camilla cleared her throat and licked at the corner of her mouth.

"Well, you've been such a good stranger."

Hunter's deep laugh caressed Camilla's hot skin. Forcefully, Camilla pulled her eyes away from him to address the waiter. "Same check," she responded, confident in her initial approach. Why she felt the need to cater to him was beyond her.

But it felt pleasant, strange, but naughty. Why, Camilla had no clue. Maybe it was the easy flow of their conversation. Or maybe it was how comfortable she felt in his presence. Or maybe it was the way Hunter licked her fingers, and Camilla was just horny. Whichever it was, Camilla was content with it all. And that was just plain ol' weird.

The server reached for her offered Visa, but Hunter was quicker, retrieving the Visa card from the server's fingers and slipping his American Express in its place.

"Excuse me," Camilla said. "What do you think you're doing?"

The server glanced between them, and Hunter nodded. The server didn't need to be told twice as he turned to clear the check.

"Not on my watch," Hunter said.

They stared at each other, Hunter taking in the soft curves of Camilla's eyes, nose, lips, and chin. Camilla reached for her briefcase.

"In that case, I'll get on with my day. Thank you for breakfast, Hunter." Camilla stood to her feet.

"Wait, I didn't get your number, and you never answered my question."

Camilla smiled and eased away from her chair. "I'm sure I'll see you around." She turned and strolled off, leaving Hunter with a whirlwind of emotions.

Chapter Three

$\mathcal{H}$unter was out of his seat, his long strides moving to chase Camilla down.

"Sir!" The server called, halting him in his steps. "Your card, sir." The server closed in on Hunter with a quick trot and a hand held out.

Hunter retrieved the plastic. "Thank you," he said, turning to take his leave.

"You're welcome, have a good day," the server called at Hunter's back.

Hunter strolled out of the restaurant across the lobby through the revolving doors into Chicago's cool temperatures. He pulled a pair of aviator glasses out and sat them on his face, hiding his retinas from the beating sun's rays. Hunter glanced left, then right and saw no signs of Camilla. She'd made her exit quickly, and he couldn't figure out how when he'd only been a few meager steps behind her.

"Can I get your car, Mr. Valentine?" Robert, the valet attendant asked.

"Robert, did you get a car for a woman just a second ago? Brown skin, shoulder length hair, brown eyes, hourglass figure. She was wearing a pinstriped suit."

Robert smiled. "That sounds like quite a woman. Unfortunately, I didn't get a car for her."

Hunter grimaced.

"However, I did see her walking down the street that way." Robert pointed.

Hunter's grimace turned into a charming smile. "My man," Hunter said, slapping Robert on the shoulder. Hunter jogged down the street.

"I'll get your car!" Robert called after him.

"You do that!" Hunter barked back.

Hunter had taken off into a sprint to meet up with the lovely Camilla. There wasn't an explanation for his excursion, other than his curiosity of her, but either way, he wasn't looking for clarification.

Robert trudged off and returned within seconds with Hunter's vehicle while Hunter was at the corner searching with laser-like vision for his mystery woman. With people walking up and down the sidewalk, Hunter's eyes darted from head to head then he cursed when his search came up empty.

Returning to The Regency, Hunter pulled out his wallet to add his American Express card back inside the bill folder. It was then that he noticed two cards in his hand. Camilla's Visa was one of them. An elaborate smile cruised across his lips. He'd removed her card from the server's hand, but

Camilla had been in such a rush to escape him, she'd left it behind.

"Must be my lucky day," Hunter drawled. He removed some cash and stuck a fifty-dollar bill in Robert's shirt pocket then jumped in his car with a whistle on his tongue.

"Go get her, tiger," Robert said, knowing all too well if Hunter Valentine was after you, there was no getting away from him. It was rare that Hunter gave chase to anyone, but on an occasion or two, he did, and Hunter always got his woman. This time, she'd slipped through his fingers, and although he wanted to brush it off and go about his day, the plastic inside his wallet gave him another reason to seek her out.

"Camilla…" he drawled, twirling her name around his tongue. Hunter left downtown headed for the manufacturing district of Chicago. February had proven to be one of the coldest months in this winter season, even going so far as leaving six inches of snow just weeks ago. However, it would be difficult to tell by the lack of outerwear that Hunter neglected. He had his moments when the wind chill was so brash that he'd throw on a thin fleece and sometimes go as far as tossing a men's scarf around his shoulders. But for the most part, it was in Hunter's nature to go without. He was, after all, a hot-blooded man. His thick skin and tough exterior held him in a natural cocoon of warmth, so the extra layer of clothing wasn't necessary for him.

Hunter pulled up to a red light just as his phone rang. The Bluetooth was attached to his internal speakers along with his caller ID that streamed across his dashboard screen.

He smirked and hit a button on his steering wheel that answered the call.

"I don't think anyone in the world is as prompt as you," he said.

A female voice chuckled. "Well when you're dealing with a celebrity such as yourself, promptness is a must," she said.

Hunter smiled. "What can I do for you this week, Ms. Tamara?"

Tamara Jenkins smiled into the receiver. "Oh, come now, you know what I want," she cooed.

Hunter lifted a brow. "I play at your jazz club every week. Do you think I'd skip one?"

Tamara gave a low throaty chuckle. "Who said anything about playing jazz?"

Hunter's smile stretched and he turned the corner, making his way to VFC Energy.

"No jazz," he asked.

"Sure, there's always that, but there's also something a little more."

"Why, Ms. Tamara, I'm flattered," Hunter said.

Tamara chuckled. "You are no stranger to flattery, I know better than that."

Hunter laughed at his long-time friend, or rather, his mother's long-time friend. Ms. Tamara Jenkins was a spicy sixty-four-year-old woman who owned Velvet Café, a jazz club in the downtown district. Every Wednesday night, Hunter would make his appearance but only in the background. As he played the mellow sounds of the saxophone behind the curtain, the poet on stage would speak the words that flowed from their heart. Sometimes Hunter would switch it up and play the piano. The instrument depended on the tone of the artist and what they were looking for.

"Now, Ms. Tamara, you know Darrell would kill me if he knew we were having this conversation," Hunter drawled.

"Oh, don't pay that ol' fool no never mind," Tamara said about one of the many sponsors that frequented the club and had his eye on Tamara. "I bet he couldn't rock my world if we were on a rollercoaster."

Hunter guffawed as he pulled into his assigned parking spot in front of the building.

"Anyway, when you're ready to stop chasing those snick-erdoodles around, you know where to find mama," she said, instantly ending their call.

Hunter chuckled some more. Ms. Tamara was right, Hunter wasn't a stranger to flattery, but it still tripped him out every time Ms. Tamara came on to him. For Hunter, it was all fun and games, which he brushed off after every incident. Opening the car to his Lexus Jeep, Hunter stepped out, pulling his tall frame to a stand. He shut the door and checked his reflection in the car's window, oblivious to the sharp winds that cruised around him. Satisfied with his look, Hunter strolled inside the building and spoke to security on his way up to his office.

"Good morning, Mr. Valentine," Harold the officer spoke with a bright smile.

"Good morning, Harold," Hunter responded, noticing the extra beam in Harold's smile. "Good news today?"

"The wife is having me a son," Harold excitedly announced.

Hunter stopped his stroll and turned back to the officer. He marched up to Harold with his hand held out. "Congratulations!" Hunter said. The two men shook hands strong and vibrantly.

"Thank you, sir, I'm pretty excited about it."

"No doubt," Hunter exclaimed. "When is she due?"

"You wouldn't believe it if I told you." At Hunter's arched brown, Harold stated, "Fourth of July."

Another spectacular smile cruised across Hunter's face. "That's a wonderful time to have a baby."

"You think so?"

"Yeah, listen, man, lunch is on me. I'll be back shortly to take care of you."

"Oh, that's not necessary," Harold cajoled.

"Sure, it is." Hunter slapped Harold on the back and strolled back to the open elevator. "I'll see you in a little bit."

"Thank you, sir!" Harold said as the elevator doors closed.

"A baby on the fourth of July," Hunter mumbled to himself. He smiled and mulled over the thought of a little Hunter Valentine running around his penthouse. It was the one thing that would completely melt his heart. For a long time, Hunter had wanted a son, or two, or three. But with his bachelor lifestyle, there was no way he could allow it to happen. The option of surrogacy had crossed his mind in the past. With an air-tight contract, Hunter could be the father of a beautiful little boy. But he wanted more than that. His son would need a mother, someone beautiful, bright, and colorful. Camilla's image strolled through his mind just as the elevator opened on his floor.

As he walked, thoughts of Camilla's lips latching onto the utensil he'd held in front of her caused heated chills to settle on his skin. The sensual way her mouth moved, and the soft ballad of her moan caused Hunter's manhood to leap in his pants. Enthused by her, Hunter immediately felt the need to taste her skin and indulge in her dessert. But what he couldn't have right then and there would have to settle for something else. So, when Camilla decided to return the favor, Hunter's *no hands* gesture had come quickly, without a second thought.

Hunter was in such a daze that he didn't hear his assistant Liza speak to him as he passed her desk. Liza peered at him with a frown. In the fourteen years Liza Crenshaw worked for Hunter, he'd never entered the building without speaking to her. This told Liza that Hunter was either off his game or something was wrong. For that reason, she stood and sauntered around her desk, walking the few feet to Hunter's office.

"Hey, boss, is everything okay?"

Hunter blinked then turned around to face her.

"Yes, everything's fine, why do you ask?" His voice was smooth and reassuring.

"You just seemed a bit off is all."

"Off?" He peered at her with that potent stare that always seared her skin.

Liza tweaked her collar nervously. It didn't matter that she'd been working with Hunter forever, there was no pill to take that would calm her nerves whenever his dark gaze met up with hers.

"I didn't hear you speak back when you came in," she pointed out.

"Oh." Hunter smiled, with a beautiful charismatic pull of his lips. "I apologize, Liza. I was in another world. How are you this morning?"

Satisfied with his attention, Liza smiled back. "Everything's great. Did you hear, ol' Harold Massingale is having a baby boy soon. Isn't that awesome? 54 years old and still going strong."

Hunter nodded and just that quick his thoughts returned to Camilla.

"Yeah..." he drawled.

A quick knock at the door turned both of their attention to the newcomer. Devin, Hunter's friend and COO, stood at the entry.

"We're all meeting up in the boardroom," he said. "Oh, and it looks like you made headlines again."

"Me, or we?" Hunter asked.

"You mainly, but there is the mention of VFC's ribbon-cutting ceremony, and the new anchor position has been filled."

Hunter tried not to groan. WTZB had been looking to fill that position for months now. They'd had billboards, commercial segments, and radio segments calling for Chicago's greatest journalists to come out and apply. But Hunter knew a fresh face and new attitude reporting on him could be good and bad, especially if the reporter wasn't a fan.

"How bad is it?" Hunter asked.

Devin nodded at the flat screen TV on Hunter's wall. Liza strolled to the remote that sat on his desk and turned the high definition television on. It was already on the local news station from a previous streaming.

When Camilla's angelic face lit up the screen, Hunter's heartbeat knocked against the wall of his chest, and his blood warmed simultaneously. His gaze dropped, and his pulse inexplicably accelerated.

"Well, I'll be damned," he said.

Chapter Four

*C*amilla watched the news segment she'd just done on Hunter Valentine through the television in the studio backroom. She tugged at her blouse and took a sip of water and tried to calm her nerves. When she arrived at WTZB, the energy in the studio was bustling. Her already uplifting morning was brightened even more when she met with Allison Sullivan the assignment editor.

Allison was all smiles, and after their initial greetings, Camilla followed Allison to the newsroom, and they'd gotten started right away. The day's local stories, along with a few national ones, were the topic of the morning's segment. Sitting in front of the camera and being the face of the station was natural for Camilla. But, as soon as she realized one of the local stories covered Hunter Valentine, a sweeping cast of perspiration sailed across her forehead. Her tone changed completely from bright to staggered, and a swarm of butterflies fluttered in her stomach. Allison sensed her nervousness, and with a calming voice, she reassured Camilla that she would be fine.

Camilla wished she could believe her, but as she spoke about Hunter's ribbon-cutting ceremony, thoughts of their naughty breakfast came to mind. The slow and sensual covering of his mouth to her fingers. The poignant way he sucked each one, leaving a heated trail of nerves slipping down her arm. All she could see was his mouth, his deep brown eyes, and the wetness of his tongue. Camilla's cheeks flushed, and she was sure sweat beads assaulted her face under the scrutiny of the studio lights. The cameras continued to roll, and as if Camilla had been a part of the WTZB team for years, she smiled into the live recording and laughed when her co-anchor Gerald Meyers cracked lighthearted jokes.

Now watching the playback, thoughts of Hunter continued, and Camilla had to wonder if she'd ever get him out of her mind. When he offered up the forkful of the heated omelet, Camilla should've declined and told him to have a good day. But, as if she weren't herself, she welcomed the offering and pushed forward against her better judgment. Camilla was sure Hunter probably thought she was another conquest he could seek out and conquer. But she wasn't, and every time Camilla wondered about the strange chemistry she'd felt with him that morning, her ex Steven called, reminding Camilla why she wasn't on the market for love. With a man like Hunter Valentine, Camilla was sure love was the last thing on his mind; more like kinky sex and sinful foreplay. That last thought made Camilla tighten her thighs and cross her legs. *Get your mind off Hunter.*

"That was fantastic. You're a natural," Allison said as the segment faded to black.

Camilla smiled over at her. Allison was in her late-thirties, and she reminded Camilla of her best friend Corinne. Allison even had the short haircut that showed off her long mahogany neck and the feminine curves in her jawline. For that reason, it was easy to be comfortable around her, and Camilla's eyes lit up at Allison's compliment.

"Do you really think so?" Camilla asked.

"Oh yes, check out our social media page. People are talking about the beautiful new anchor at WTZB."

"Beautiful?" Camilla countered, reaching across the table to retrieve the iPad from Allison's hand.

Allison snickered. "Their words, not mine."

Camilla took her eyes down WTZB's Facebook page.

"Great job with the new anchor!" One comment said. "Easy on the eyes, I could watch her every morning regardless of what she's talking about," another commenter said. Camilla frowned and tapped his picture which in turn maximized his Facebook page. The commenter was a middle-aged white male with a receding hairline.

"Some old freaks on here," Camilla mumbled. Allison burst into laughter. Mortified that she'd been heard, Camilla covered her mouth and slid the iPad back to Allison. "I apologize," she said.

Allison waved her off. "No need for an apology," Allison said as her laughter retreated. "You're right. You'd be surprised how many are single, lonely, or divorced men just looking for a cute face with their morning weather."

"I would like to say I'm used to this sort of thing, but I never got into the social media craze back in Miami."

"Ah, I see. Do you miss home?"

Camilla brightened again. "Not yet."

Allison nodded.

"Check back with me in a few months though."

"I'll do that." Allison glanced over at the clock on the wall. "Do you have plans for lunch?"

"Not one. In fact, it would probably take me the entire hour to figure out where to eat."

"I've got you covered if you don't mind some company."

"That would be great. Let's do it."

Camilla and Allison removed their earpieces and left the newsroom. As they trailed down the hall, a voice called out to Camilla.

"Mrs. Augustina."

Camilla turned back to see her co-anchor Gerald Meyers approaching. She offered him a soft smile and corrected his salutation.

"Miss," she said.

"Oh yes, my apologies."

"That's quite alright."

"I wanted to congratulate you."

"For?"

"You did wonderful this morning. You'll be a great asset to WTZB."

Gerald Meyers was a fifty-something white male with a head full of silver-white hair and a groomed gray mustache.

Camilla could tell he was a regular at the gym by the way his solid arms stood out in his button-down Neiman Marcus shirt.

A pleasant smile cornered Camilla's lush lips. "Thank you. That means a lot coming from someone with as much seniority as you."

"I'm only speaking the truth. I look forward to working with you more, Ms. Augustina."

"You too," Camilla chirped. "I'll see you after lunch."

"Indeed."

Camilla turned to continue behind Allison, but she had a feeling Gerald was still looking after her. Wanting to dispel the notion, she glanced back over her shoulder and found him lingering in the hall watching her.

Camilla sighed. The last thing she wanted was any romantic thoughts or suggestions running rampant in her co-anchor's head. It was okay to be attracted to someone, so for now, Camilla put it out of her mind as she and Allison made their way to a diner across the street.

"This is perfect," Camilla said once they were seated. She removed her Eddie Bauer quilted winter coat and let it hang on the back of her chair.

"This is my go-to spot when I don't have much time to go anywhere else, or when it's so cold outside I can't stand to be in the weather longer than a minute."

Camilla nodded with a chuckle. "Completely under-standable."

"And just so you know, yes, Gerald hits on every pretty face that walks into the office. But he's harmless and we all just pay him no mind."

"Good to know."

"He's got a thing for chocolate-skinned women."

"Into the swirl love, huh?" Camilla retorted.

This time, Allison chuckled and nodded. "He doesn't discriminate, that's for sure."

The ladies chuckled again, and somehow Camilla couldn't help but point out this morning's news.

"So, a lot of happenings going on in Chicago, huh?"

"There's always something going on in the windy city."

"I can tell. Is Hunter Valentine a big deal here?"

Allison's eyes twinkled at the mention of Hunter Valentine.

"The biggest," she said.

"Really, how so?"

"Okay, let me take that back. One of the biggest. I'd say his entire family is a big deal, and then there is the Rose family. They're a pretty big deal, too."

"I think I saw one of them on a billboard when I left the airport last night. Something about needing a lawyer."

"Oh yeah, that's Jordan. He's co-owner of Rose and Garnett LLC. He and Hunter are rivals. Men," Allison said, "sometimes they never grow up."

"Hmmm," Camilla said. "Why are they rivals?"

"I really don't know, but it's been this long going feud, and every time any one of our cameras gets close to Jordan or Hunter, they clam up and go silent on us."

"Sounds like a day in the life of a reporter."

Allison chuckled "Exactly. Anyway, the most I can tell you about Hunter is what I've witnessed or reported on."

Camilla waited patiently for Allison to go on.

"He's a ladies' man for sure."

Camilla thought about the women she'd seen leaving his place that morning. Three of them. At the time, she didn't care much about it, but now it made her sick.

"That I can believe," Camilla added dryly.

"How do you mean?"

Camilla stuttered. "I—uh, don't deny he's a lady-killer. I mean, I'd have to be blind not to notice how attractive he is."

Allison nodded just as a waitress sidled up to their table.

"Good afternoon, ladies, I'm Charmaine, I'll be your server for today. Seen anything yummy on the menu or would you like any suggestions?"

"I think I'll take a turkey sandwich with the works—tomato, lettuce, cheese and French fries," Allison said. "Oh, and a sweet tea."

The waitress entered her information in a smart device she held. "Anything else?"

"That's it."

"And for you?" Charmaine turned to Camilla.

"I think I'll have the same. That sounded pretty good although I probably won't eat many of the French fries, or they may just put me to sleep."

The three of them chuckled.

"I've got you down. Be back shortly with your orders."

"Thank you," Camilla and Allison chimed.

"As I was saying," Allison continued, "yes, Hunter Valentine is notorious for having a different lady on his arm, and all the women swoon over him but swear if they ever encountered him, they wouldn't give him the time of day."

"And you don't believe them?"

A single arched brow on Allison's face lifted. "Are you kidding me? They want to appear as if they wouldn't be interested because he's the head of playboy academy, but I know better. And deep down they do, too. Hunter is fine as hell, and besides that, he's about his business. If a woman could be on his arm even for a night, she'd rather toss her friend in a cage full of pit bulls than deny an evening with him."

"That serious, huh?" Camilla wasn't impressed. Hunter sounded like the kind of chauvinist that she'd rather avoid at all cost. And yet, the feeling of submission that she felt earlier still rattled her.

"Stick around long enough, and you'll see what I mean."

"I'm not sure I want too," Camilla retorted.

Allison laughed. "Unhuh, that's what they all say."

Camilla took her gaze around the restaurant in desperate need to shuffle her thoughts and change the subject.

"So, when we get back, is there anything specific I need to know?"

"We'll go through and pick out the reports for the two o'clock news cycle."

The waitress returned promptly with their orders.

"This looks delicious," Camilla pointed out.

"It is. Haven't met a turkey sandwich in all of Chicago that was better."

Camilla giggled and said a small prayer over her food.

"Are you a religious woman?" Allison asked.

Camilla glanced at her just as she lifted the sandwich to

her mouth. Removing it slightly, she responded. "I wouldn't say religious. I believe that Jesus Christ died for my sins, and for that I'm grateful."

"Hmmm," Allison said.

"I take it you don't," Camilla said.

"Oh, nothing like that." Allison waved her off. "I grew up a Jehovah's Witness. "But I've been converted for say, about five years now. The differences of the religion pique my interest all the time."

Camilla's eyes rose. "A new Christian. Nice."

"Yeah, I wouldn't say that I sin any less but," Allison shrugged, and Camilla laughed loudly.

"Hey, I've been a Christian for most of my life, and I can say the same. Here's to no judgment and navigating this thing called life the best we can." Camilla lifted her glass for a toast, and Allison followed suit.

"I will definitely drink to that."

The ladies continued their conversation over the next half hour until it was time to head back to the station. The waitress moseyed to the table to collect their bills.

"I hope everything was to your liking," Charmaine said.

"Yes, it was great," they both said.

"That's good to hear. Will this be separate checks or?"

"Two checks," Camilla chimed as she searched relentlessly for her Visa. She dug into her bill folder and shifted through each pocket finding it missing. A frown covered her face.

"Something wrong?" Allison asked.

"I think I may have slipped my card in my jacket pocket by mistake. Probably in a rush or something." Camilla searched her Eddie Bauer coat and came up emptyhanded. Her thoughts shuffled as she tried to remember the last time she'd used her card.

The Breakfast Hut. Hunter had taken it out of the server's hand and slipped his card into its place to pay for their food.

"Shit," Camilla cursed. "I'm sorry, I seem to have left it at the restaurant I had breakfast at this morning. Is it possible—"

"Not a big deal at all, just pay me back tomorrow." Allison glanced up at Charmaine. "One check please."

"Thank you. I'll have it first thing."

Camilla sighed and wondered how she would get her card back from Hunter. She would have to knock on his door once she got home and that would blow her cover. As it stood, Hunter didn't know she was the only other occupant on his floor, and Camilla wanted to keep it that way. A population of chills settled across her skin as she thought about them meeting again. Camilla knew she'd have to give herself a serious pep talk to stay focused.

Chapter Five

"Good evening, Madame," Robert the valet attendant spoke.

"Good evening," Camilla responded. "How was your day?"

"Oh, I can't complain. How about yours?"

"I'd say it was a win," Camilla smiled easily.

"Good, good," Robert repeated.

"I'm surprised you're still here. Do you usually work this late?"

Camilla snagged a look at her wristwatch. It was six p.m., and when she'd left this morning it was before eight.

"Picking up some extra hours. I'll be long gone in the next two."

"Oh, in that case…" Camilla handed over her keys.

"Don't mind if I do. Thank you, pretty lady."

Camilla removed her handbag and sauntered through

the revolving doors of The Regency. The luxurious layout of the building was one of the things besides security that sold Camilla on the building. From the multi-pendant crystal chandelier that hung two stories from a coffered ceiling, to the wenge flooring, oversized tufted ottomans, and contemporary furniture, the high-rise was built like a palace, and a girl could only dream. With fingers crossed, Camilla strutted to The Breakfast Hut. Once she arrived, her fears had been answered. They were closed.

"Of course, they're closed, Camilla. They're a breakfast restaurant," she said, scolding herself.

Completing an about-face, Camilla strolled back to the lobby and sauntered up to the receptionist desk. This was another great feature of the building. There was always someone there twenty-four hours to answer any and all concerns.

The brunette sitting behind the marble countertop appeared to be Camilla's age, and she clicked away at her keyboard as she kept her eyes focused on whatever was on the monitor in front of her. Camilla cleared her throat, and the lady glanced up then smiled. She pushed her glasses up her nose, and they slid slightly down again.

"Good evening, I'm Sonya, how can I help you?"

"Sonya, I'm new to the building, just rented the mini penthouse suite. Unfortunately, this morning, I left my credit card in The Breakfast Hut in a rush to get to work." *More like in a rush to run from Hunter.* Camilla made sure not to roll her eyes at that last thought. "I was wondering if maybe one of the servers or even the manager might have left it here."

Camilla held her breath, and Sonya frowned. "Give me just a moment, and I'll check," she said.

"Thank you."

Sonya stood and moseyed to the backroom. While Camilla waited, she pulled out her iPhone and scrolled through her notifications. Four missed calls and an equal amount of text messages from none other than Steven. Camilla shook her head. The man never gave up; he was like a thorn in Camilla's backside. She was never answering his phone call, and if the world ended before Camilla ever saw Steven again, it wouldn't be soon enough.

Sonya reappeared, and Camilla saw no evidence of her Visa.

"I'm sorry, but it doesn't look like we've received a credit card from The Breakfast Hut. If you'd like, I can leave a message for the manager, and she'll return your call as soon as she's available."

Camilla let go of the breath she was holding. "That's fine," she said, but she felt the opposite.

"Okay, let me have your telephone number and your full name."

Camilla rattled off the information while her skin turned hot simultaneously. She would have to face Hunter again, regardless of how much she'd rather not. *You're a grown woman, Camilla, you can handle it.*

"I've got you down," Sonya said, pushing her glasses back up her nose again.

"Thank you."

Camilla turned and left, headed for the elevators. As she walked, each step she took felt as if she were stepping in quicksand. She fought mightily to take another. Reaching the steel box, Camilla lifted her hand for the button just as the elevator dinged and the doors parted. The unexpected sound rattled her, and she jumped slightly as a woman with short blonde curls and blue eyes rushed from inside.

"Excuse me," she said as she shot past Camilla.

Camilla covered her chest and removed herself from the woman's path as she practically skipped past her. Clearly, the woman wasn't looking for a response since she was at the exit before Camilla could get settled into the confines of the elevator. The doors closed, and Camilla dropped her hand, deciding now was the time to have a one-on-one with herself.

"You are thinking too hard about this," she said. "You're simply going to retrieve your card. You know he has it. He knows he has it, and it belongs to you."

Camilla paused.

"So, what if you couldn't control yourself over breakfast? That was then, and you've had all day to get over it, so just do it."

Allison's words came back to haunt Camilla.

"They want to appear as if they wouldn't be interested because he's the head of playboy academy, but I know better. And deep down they do, too. Hunter is fine as hell, and besides that, he's about his business. If a woman could be on his arm even for a night, she'd rather toss her friend in a cage full of pit bulls than deny an evening with him. Stick around long enough and you'll see what I mean."

Camilla rubbed her hands together and collected herself. When the doors opened on their floor, she peeped her head out to see if anyone else was lingering around. The last thing she wanted to do was run into one of his overnight escapades. *Ugh.* Stepping off the elevator, she held her chin up with confidence and strolled down the hallway to his door. There she stood in front of it, staring at the cherry oak wood frame. Taking in a deep breath, Camilla lifted her hand to knock quickly, but instead, she paused when her heart picked up an extra beat. Her hand faltered, and she tried to shake it off but as it rose again to knock, Camilla's pulse quickened.

What was happening to her? Camilla dropped her hand again and continued to stare at the door as if it was an abominable opponent she needed to size up to figure out how best to take it on head first. Her legs moved backward, and Camilla retreated. With haste, she dug her hand into her purse and fished for her keys.

"Why didn't you have your keys ready, Camilla," she scolded.

But she knew why. Her focus had been on Hunter and nothing else. When her fingers swept across the bottom and scooped up the chain, Camilla breathed a sigh of relief. She entered them into the lock and pushed the door, stepping inside the safety of her abode. She turned and shut the panel, letting her back fall against the solid grain of it.

"What is wrong with you?" She asked to only herself.

Pushing off, Camilla turned and leaned her face toward the peephole, checking for any signs of movement outside. When her inspection came up empty, she sighed, and her head fell back as her eyes closed tight. Camilla never felt so ridiculous. She'd been in Chicago all of twenty-four hours and only been in Hunter's presence, what, thirty minutes?

And he'd managed to stir up a commotion so thoroughly Camilla thought she might seize up.

"It's not that serious, Camilla," she said.

Tossing her handbag on the entryway table stand, Camilla strolled to the kitchen and shed her coat. The thick jacket went flying onto the countertop as Camilla searched the cabinet for the complimentary bottle of wine she'd received upon leasing the expensive suite.

"This is more like it," she said, reaching in for the bottle.

The smile on Camilla's face faltered when she noticed a cork but wasn't in the vicinity of a corkscrew. A curse left her lips, and she almost slammed the bottle onto the counter. An unnerved, high-pitched laugh escaped her lips as she leaned a curvaceous hip into the edge. *Go to him.* Camilla rubbed her temples.

"He'll wonder how I knew where he lived," she argued with herself. "Then, what will I tell him?"

Camilla held there as if waiting for a response from herself.

"This is crazy."

She pushed off the counter and strolled back to her front door, determined. Truth be told, Camilla didn't have to tell him a thing. He had her Visa card and he needed to give it back. If Hunter asked how she found out where he lived, she'd just simply shrug and ask him to return what rightfully belonged to her.

Camilla nodded as if making up her mind that, that explanation would do. She swung her door open and closed it behind her without taking the time to grab her key and lock it as she exited. As she closed in on his door again,

Camilla paused, and a fleeting thought sailed through her mind.

What if he has company?

That would be embarrassing. But he wouldn't know that, after all, Camilla was just there to get what was hers. So, without another thought, she took her knuckles across the solid wooden beam in three taps. Her pulse quickened again as she waited, feeling anxious and antsy at the same time.

Camilla turned to glance down the hall then back up again, but there was no answer at his door. Pulling her wrist to her face, she glanced at the time. It had only been an hour since she'd arrived, but it felt like two. Camilla knocked again, this time a little harder. The walls were pretty thick, so it was only right that the door would be, too.

Without trying, Camilla found herself leaning into the door, placing an ear against it to listen to see if there was any movement inside. Hunter picked that moment to answer the door, and when it swung open, a flow of air pushed Camilla forward, causing her to collide with the solid expanse of his bare chest.

"Oh, my goodness," Camilla yelped as Hunter's stern hands reached out to hold her steady.

"Camilla," he said, surprised. The connection of their touch caused a ripple of heat to slip over them both; further proving that the chemistry from earlier that morning was not a fluke.

Camilla's eyes slowly trailed up the length of his granite-solid chest. They cruised up over the muscles in his shoulders past the pillar of his throat, masculine jaw, kissable lips, and thick nose into the depths of his stinging gaze. She was frozen there, unmoving and unwavering. Her thoughts weren't jumbled but set on a singular highlight. His face.

Hunter was the most beautiful man Camilla had ever seen. And by beautiful she meant exquisitely carved as each plane and surface on his face was shaped for the perfection of his mouth, nose, eyes, and ears. The divinity in which he was created must have been one of the biggest masterpieces God had ever molded.

And yet… Hunter was thinking much the same.

As they continued to stare at one another, their breaths mingled as they took in each distinct proportion of their features. Hunter admired the sharp cut in her feline eyes and how her brown orbs accentuated her sienna skin. Her nose sat sleek with a sexy upturn at the end, and the mole just above her lush mouth added to the allure of her divine characteristics. His eyes drove down the arc of her neck and covered her feminine shoulders, hefty breasts, and curvaceous thighs that were dispensed into the pinstripe skirt he'd seen her in earlier.

His eyes darkened as a blaze of heat crawled up his skin. Hunter's hand moved to her chin, and his finger grazed alongside the curve of it.

"Angel…" he said, his voice deep and nocturnal.

An involuntary shiver trembled from Camilla, and as if snapping out of her trance, she pushed off his chest and took a step back. Their disconnection left them both feeling at odds, but they both forced themselves to hold firm to their stance.

"Hunter," Camilla said finally. His lids dropped even

more as if his name slipping from her tongue cast a turbulence through him. She cleared her throat. "I didn't mean to interrupt, but you have something that belongs to me."

Hunter knew what she wanted, but he was inclined not to give it to her right away. After all, Camilla had been on his mind all day, and he had gone over every scenario of how he could meet up with her again. His heavy lids blinked, and he stepped to the side and opened the door wider.

"Come in," he said.

Camilla swallowed thickly and almost shook her head off her shoulders.

"No, thank you, I just stopped by to get my credit card. You do have it, don't you?"

A gradual smile tapered across his magnificent mouth.

"I do, but I won't leave you standing in the hallway while I retrieve it."

"Oh, I don't mind."

They eyed each other for a long second before Hunter spoke again.

"Are you afraid to be alone with me, Angel?"

Camilla held strong, even as another storm of heat settled over her from his endearment. Her immediate response was supposed to be, *My name is Camilla.* But for some reason, she stopped the reprimand and responded, "Don't be ridiculous. I'm not scared of you. I took taekwondo in college and excelled as a black belt. I could take you down, if I wanted too, but I'm not into hurting my neighbors."

Camilla noticed as soon as the words slipped from her

lips that she'd divulged too much information. Hunter, on the other hand, was more intrigued now than he had been when he met her this morning. His eyes roamed down the hallway to the mini penthouse suite then swept back to her gorgeous face, pinning her with a sharp gaze. Once again, he covered her entire body with a glance, and Camilla pursed her lips tightly, making sure not to speak.

"A black belt." Hunter nodded with a smirk. "Why don't you show me some of your moves?"

Another riveting flush of heat sailed over Camilla, and her cheeks reddened. She opened her mouth for a spicy retort but found none. Hunter found it amusing that she'd gone mute on him. His eyes fell to the bottle of Opus One Napa in her hand.

"Are you in need of a corkscrew," he asked.

Camilla had almost forgotten it was in her hand.

"Um," she faltered.

"Please, come inside. You have the tools you need should I get out of line, but just so you know, I wouldn't dare."

Don't do it, girl. Stand your ground.

"Only for a minute. I have work in the morning, and I need to prepare," she heard herself saying.

Pleased, Hunter nodded. "Of course."

Camilla coached her feet to move, and with a sensual sway in her hips, she cruised inside.

Chapter Six

$\mathcal{E}$ntering Hunter's home was like stepping through a vortex that led to another dimension. Camilla took her eyes over the expanse of the living area, and her mouth parted on a gasp. Hunter's walls were designed like a living mural like that of a TV show set. Camilla floated deeper into the room, and with each step, her feet sank into a gray plush shag carpet. It caused her to pause then glance down, and suddenly, she felt the need to take off her heels, so she did. As Camilla balanced herself on one foot, she reached down with the other and removed one shoe. When she shifted to take off the other, Hunter was at her side.

"Here, allow me," his deep voice thundered. His arm slipped around her waist and held her firm as he slid the other shoe off her foot. "Better," he asked.

"Much."

An easy smile trekked across his face, and for a second,

Camilla almost forgot about the journey she was on as her body melted in response to his touch. They stared each other head-on, then Camilla blinked, and the wall canvas recaptured her attention.

Hunter reached for the Opus One Napa. "I'll hold on to this for you."

She let him take it, and he removed his hold on her, allowing Camilla to continue her voyage to the mural.

On one side, men played basketball on a court. Three on three, one of them looking oddly like Hunter. Camilla walked the length of the wall, haphazardly driving her fingertips across the images as she moved. The scene changed with each step she took. An older man with a bald head and a long gray thin beard sat at a table playing chess with a more frustrated, younger looking brother. Camilla peered closer at the image.

"Is that you?" she asked.

"It is."

Hunter offered no further explanation, and Camilla didn't expand on her thoughts of the scene. It was clear, the young man wasn't winning the game, and again five other younger men stood off to the background with an outburst of laughter written all over their faces. Camilla stood with a smile, and then she moved on to the next image. A garden with an abundance of beautiful blooming flowers with blue skies and a beaming sun in the backdrop trailed down his hallway. It hadn't dawned on Camilla that she'd left his living area and was now sauntering deeper into Hunter's space.

"Are you certain you want to go back there," his voice drummed.

Camilla halted her steps just as her eyes traveled over a single word written across the sky of the mural, Trevor. She blinked and rotated slowly on her bare feet.

"I'm sorry, I didn't mean to pry. Your wall is captivating."

Hunter smiled easily as he stood with his hands thrown inside of his pants pockets. Camilla's eyes roamed over the pecs in his chest, and she'd almost wondered how she was able to take her eyes off his excellence.

She blinked and went to speak again when a light in her peripheral caught her attention. Turning toward the opposing side of the wall came with another magnificent delight. Instead of a wall, there was a sweeping view of Chicago's skyscrapers behind a thick pane of window glass. A light stood off in the distance on top of another building just across the way. Camilla's eyes bulged as she moved closer to the barrier of glass that ran from the room she'd just left, past her, and down the hallway before disappearing around a corner she'd yet to venture into. She'd been so taken with the mural that Camilla failed to notice the view.

"Why do I suddenly feel cheated," she mumbled. "This is amazing. I would've paid..." her words faltered. "I mean I would've sold an arm and both legs if it was needed to pay for a view as spectacular as this."

"You may have needed a full body, and that would only cover the deposit," his sexy voice grooved.

Camilla smiled, somehow knowing that he was right.

"Is it possible that the building has another view like

this, that's available for rent?"

Hunter ventured closer to Camilla. He'd watched her from afar as she trailed, mesmerized by his memorial. He took special note of the way her pecan eyes lit up and her beautiful lips parted as she assessed the detail on it. It wasn't the only thing he'd noticed; the sexy way her hips moved each time she placed one foot in front of the other, and the curve of her derriere and the soft sway of her mane as she progressed.

Hunter had seen beautiful women from different countries across the globe; exotic and racy, that hailed from different tribes. But here in his own backyard, he'd found a rare diamond; as if she was a mixture of all of those beautiful faces combined into an original chef-d'oeuvre. He wanted to know her, and it wasn't a matter of a possibility. His first step to making sure it would happen was getting her inside his suite. So, when she declined, Hunter pushed forward, with no plans on letting up. Now she was in his lion's den, and Hunter wanted to make sure being here made her want to return, again and again.

Closing the distance, Hunter stood over Camilla and answered her question.

"There's not a view of this magnitude, but there is one on a lower level. I'm not sure if it would tickle your fancy, but let me check with the building owner, and I can get back to you."

"Really?"

Hunter smiled again. The way her eyes twinkled when she was excited was becoming his favorite thing to watch.

"For sure," he responded. He pulled his bottom lip in

with his teeth, and Camilla's eyes dropped to his mouth.

She shivered then glanced back toward the window then to the mural.

"Who's Trevor?"

The sparkle in Hunter's gaze dimmed, and she watched him stare at her as if deciding whether to reveal the message behind the mural.

"My brother," he said. "Have you had dinner by any chance?"

Camilla blinked at the quick turn of conversation.

"Um, no. I planned to make a salad when I got home, but I needed to get my card from you since I now owe my coworker money for lunch."

"I see."

The doorbell rang a tune that sounded throughout the penthouse.

Camilla's brows rose. "I should probably go. It wasn't my intention to interrupt your company. If you don't mind, could you—"

"Not company," his baritone voice cruised along her skin. "Dinner."

Camilla didn't speak, and she almost felt foolish that she'd assumed otherwise. Almost.

"I'd like you to stay. Have dinner with me. I hate dining alone."

Camilla smirked. Of course, he did. Hunter Valentine, alone? Oh, the horror, she thought. Her stomach rumbled, and they both heard it.

"What are you having?"

"Chicken with Beurre Blanc and dilled parsnips and

carrots. You'll love the seasoning, it's like a tango on your tongue."

Camilla was finding it extremely hard to keep everything Hunter said from being sexual. But the man made her libido overactive like nothing she'd ever felt.

"I don't usually have dinner with bare-chested men," she said.

A deep echoing guffaw spilled from Hunter's throat, and it floated over and tickled Camilla's eardrum. She squirmed, and her hands sailed down her hips as if to calm her nervous system.

Hunter nodded as his laugh subsided, leaving mirth in his soulful eyes. The doorbell rang again.

"I'll put on a shirt if you get the door," he said.

Camilla arched a brow. "You want me to answer your door?"

"Yeah."

"What if it isn't dinner, but one of your…" she paused, and this time Hunter lifted a brow.

"One of my what?"

Camilla swallowed. If she was going to keep the location of her apartment a secret, she'd have to remember to mind her tongue. Camilla couldn't very well tell him she'd seen his company leave this morning. But it was hard to do. Being around Hunter the few times they'd shared space had proven that. Even her actions were out of whack when with him.

"Nothing," she said.

Amused, Hunter reached for her hand, and a squadron of heat assaulted their flesh. Singed, they both stared at each other before Hunter tugged her toward the front room. Entering again was like entering for the first time for Camilla. It was now that she saw the black leather sectional sofa, the sleek contemporary leather chair sitting adjacent from it. Gray accessories sat quaintly around the room, and a chandelier in the shape of a multifaceted globe hung from a tray ceiling.

"I love the design of this place, it must have cost you a fortune to have it set up just the way you wanted it."

"A mini fortune," he said with a smirk. Hunter closed in on the door then reached for the handle and opened it.

"Macalister's," the older man on the other side cajoled, pronouncing the restaurant Hunter had ordered from.

"Thank you, Phillip. I'll take it from here."

Hunter pulled the cart inside and handed Phillip a tip.

"Thank you, sir."

Phillip didn't stay around to chat. He departed quickly, leaving Camilla and Hunter alone again.

"Are these blackout blinds?" Camilla questioned, still admiring Hunter's space.

"They are," he responded.

Knowing that at the push of a button his blinds would drop, sealing the room in total darkness sent a spiraling zing shooting through Camilla. Besides that thrill, she wondered why she hadn't thought to install the same feature in her suite. *Because you're not rich, and you broke the bank paying the rent.* That thought seemed to put her in her place.

"I think I envy you," she said, turning from the blinds to look at Hunter.

"Don't. You can enjoy them whenever you like. For as

long as you like."

The invitation not only surprised Camilla, but Hunter, too. Had he really just invited her to come over when it pleased her because that wasn't a request he'd bestowed upon anyone.

"Come with me," he said before either of them could think too long about the idea.

Camilla sauntered up to him, and Hunter reached for her hand and linked their fingers. They strolled down another long corridor before entering a dining area with more tray ceilings, black Italian marble floors, and luxurious surroundings. The table they approached was fit for royalty. The Lucite tabletop and modern leather chairs had a back so massive it rose seven feet; no doubt to accommodate his massive frame.

Hunter pulled out her chair, and Camilla sat. In no time, he added their dishes and her bottle of wine to the surface. She watched the way his muscles flexed as Hunter strolled around the table, and an expedition of chills found their way down her skin. Hunter removed the silver cloche, and the smell of freshly roasted chicken filled the room.

"I'll be back in just a second."

Hunter disappeared before Camilla could change her mind. Maybe she did want to have dinner with a shirtless man after all. First time for everything. Camilla shook her head. *No. Stay focused.* But it was a bit too late for that. Especially seeing as how he'd managed to have her stay for dinner. She let her fingers trail up the wine bottle and tried to shift her thinking, but at that moment, Hunter was all her mind cared to commemorate.

Chapter Seven

When Hunter returned, the magnificence of his washboard abs was hidden, but the muscles weren't held back by the garment as they pushed through the seams and teased Camilla as if he hadn't shielded himself at all. The swagger in his long stride held her in rapture, and an avalanche of heat swept down her spine.

"How's this," he asked.

Camilla nodded, not trusting her voice.

"Good, I aim to please."

Camilla smirked. Sure, he did.

Hunter disappeared around another corner and returned with champagne flutes and a corkscrew. Placing one flute in front of her, Hunter lifted the bottle and popped the cork then poured her glass halfway. She admired his thoughtfulness. He could have filled it to the top to get her drunk. But so far, Hunter had only shown sincerity, and Camilla could appreciate a man like that. He grabbed a utensil and added food to Camilla's plate than his own and took his seat while filling his own glass.

"Do you pray?" He asked.

"Yes."

"What are your religious preferences?"

Camilla smile again. *Thoughtful.*

"I'm a Christian."

"Shall we?"

Hunter reached for her hands, and they bowed their heads.

"Father God…"

As Hunter prayed for a blessing and the nourishment of their bodies and soul, Camilla found herself praying for forgiveness of having naughty thoughts as Hunter spoke at the throne.

Please Lord, forgive me, for I have sinned and can't seem to stop.

The depth in his vocals and the way Camilla's body vibrated slightly from the bass of it caused her to shift and cross her legs then repent more. She was so busy begging for forgiveness that she almost missed it when the prayer ended.

"Amen," Hunter said.

His perfectly curled lashes fluttered as he looked over at her.

"Amen," Camilla responded.

Hunter gave her hand a squeeze before releasing it and reaching for a knife and fork.

"This dish is best served if you eat it like this."

He took the knife through her chicken, cutting a corner

of it just right to fit the spear of the fork. When he had enough, Hunter dipped the food into the Beurre Blanc sauce then lifted the dish to her lips. Without dissuasion, Camilla settled her mouth over the food, and her lids fluttered at the attack on her palate.

"Good, right?"

Camilla nodded as her mind processed the flavor.

"Wow," she said finally. "That is incredible."

Retrieving her own utensils, Camilla cut into her chicken and followed his lead, dipping then taking another bite. Her eyes rolled back to a close then fluttered open and rounded to him.

"Mmmm," she moaned with a soft shake of her head. "Heavenly."

Hunter's dick bucked against his zipper, and inwardly, he told himself to calm.

"Are you going to eat?" Camilla asked, watching him stare at her mouth unflinchingly.

Hunter cut into his chicken while keeping his eyes on her.

"How was your first day on the job," he queried, dipping his chicken and taking a bite of his own.

Camilla lifted the glass of wine to her mouth and took a sip. The sweet liquor mixed with the meal so enticingly she thought about having the cuisine again tomorrow.

"It was good. The staff is great and very enthusiastic. The atmosphere is light and non-pervasive." She licked the corner of her lips, and Hunter's gaze followed her tongue. "But, I think my co-anchor has a thing for black women."

That didn't seem to surprise Hunter. Any man worth his salt would be attracted to Camilla.

"Actually, I know he does since the coworker I owe money to said as much."

Camilla made sure to put that out in the air again. Since Hunter, still, had yet to hand over her card.

"What would make your coworker tell you that?"

Camilla smiled softly. "He's a flirt. It was minor, but I can spot a flirt a mile away."

"Because you have superpowers?"

Camilla laughed an ambrosial sound that heated Hunter's skin, sending a flare to his groin.

"No, but the tell-tale signs are there."

"Hmm," Hunter's intoxicating voice grooved. "What is your coworker's name if you don't mind me asking?"

"Allison. She reminds me of my friend back in Florida, Corinne."

"Florida," he said. "The Sunshine State."

Camilla nodded. "Born and raised. Gators all day, skee-wee!" Camilla called, and a beautiful smile covered her face as she tossed up her fingers in her signature sorority hand gesture.

Hunter's eyes lit up. "You're Alpha Kappa Alpha," he pointed out.

Camilla's smile held steady. "Yeaaaah baby," she crooned, going in for another bite of her chicken Beurre blanc.

"A-Phi!" Hunter shouted, and Camilla almost choked on her food. She swallowed quickly then dabbed her mouth with a napkin.

"No way," she said, sitting forward astonished. It couldn't be possible that he was a part of the brother fraternity to her sorority.

The gorgeous smile that ran across Hunter's face was proof in the pudding.

"Yeaaaah, baby…" his thick voice drummed, repeating what she'd said in the sexiest manner Camilla had ever heard it.

"You're Alpha Phi Alpha…" she gushed.

Camilla sat back against her seat, and Hunter reached out and stroked her chin.

"I pledged because I wanted to offer positive change not only in the brotherhood, but in the Black community. I was already popular in society because of my family's reputation, so spreading positivity on a greater scale was my goal. Once I became a sophomore, I was elected Pledge Class Vice President. I held that position for another semester before I elevated to General President."

"Wow, what an advancement," Camilla said.

The corners of Hunter's succulent lips lifted, and he nodded. "True that. It was a ton of responsibility, but I was up for the challenge." His gaze lingered on her. "I've got the feeling we were destined to meet, Angel."

Camilla smirked outwardly. Inwardly, she shivered. "You think?"

"I do."

They watched each other for another long moment, Camilla taking in the sudden coincidence and Hunter wondering what else fate had in store when it came to his *Angel*.

Camilla took a sip of her wine, needing to calm herself, but it only seemed to make her even more comfortable with Hunter.

"Tell me, why did you pledge AKA?" he asked.

Camilla crossed her legs, and Hunter wanted to pat himself on the back for not looking.

"Initially, I'd watched as the sorority groomed young women to be outstanding leaders of the community. It not only sparked my interest, but it made me want to recruit more women for the sorority. But I needed to be a part of it first. Instead of jumping the gun, I did a little research. There are a lot of great ones, but Alpha Kappa Alpha stood out the most. I created a lot of friendships from being a part of it. And now that I'm long gone from college, I still recognize my sisters when I see our colors or hear our call. It's amazing that even though I may not know the individual personally, being a member connects us instantly. There have been many times when I have been in public and walked past a sister wearing our logo, and I'll shout skee-wee!" Camilla laughed, and Hunter enjoyed the serenaded sound of her voice. "We'd stopped instantly and take a selfie with each other. It's a bond like I've never experienced."

Camilla reached out and lifted the wine glass to her lips, taking a sip of the last contents. Hunter stood from his seat and poured her a little more. At her inquisitive look, he paused.

"Enough?" He asked.

Camilla mulled it over. "This should be good. I'm not a big drinker, so I can already feel it working me out." Her eyes swept over him before meeting his stare again.

"You said it's a bond like you've never experienced before," Hunter said, sitting the bottle back down and reclaiming his seat. "Are you an only child?"

Camilla didn't have a problem answering his question, but she couldn't help but remember how Hunter had instantly shifted the conversation when she inquired about Trevor.

"I'll make a deal with you. If you get to ask me about my family, I can ask you about yours."

Hunter didn't jump at her proposal right away. Instead, he let it linger there, and Camilla could tell he wasn't up for it.

"One question," he said finally.

Camilla looked him over completely. The warmness in his eyes had paused, and his jaw seemingly locked tightly.

"Yes," Camilla answered. "I'm an only child." Instead of asking the question she really wanted to know, she decided to save it for another time, if ever a time came. "The men on the mural playing basketball. Are they your friends? Brothers?"

The question seemed to make Hunter relax, and the warmness she'd gotten used to returned along with his relaxed jaw.

"They're my brothers."

"It must be nice to have siblings."

"Sometimes," he joked.

Camilla smiled. "Are you the oldest?"

Hunter smirked. "You could say that." He chuckled at her quizzical look. "We were born together. Me first by one and a half a minutes. So, I guess you can call me the oldest."

Camilla thought she'd heard wrong. "Wait, all of you!?"

"Yes. We're septuplets. Not identical. My mom is a warrior." His smile was easy.

"Oh my God, how amazing! When I first heard of the famous Octomom who had eight babies at once, I thought surely that was a rare occurrence, but seven is still… wow." Camilla thought back to the mural. There were only six of them in each drawing. "Wait," she said, going over it again in her head. *Trevor*. Camilla wanted to pry more, but she held on to it. She lifted the flute to her lips and drained the remaining contents.

"You don't mind if I have a bit more, do you," she asked. "I swear this is my last round."

"Of course. It is yours after all."

She gave him a gracious smile. Oddly, Camilla also wondered what it would be like for Hunter to be hers, too.

Chapter Eight

*T*hey were enjoying each other's company too well; that much was apparent when Camilla failed to check the time, and the minutes had turned into hours. Camilla and Hunter polished off their meals and moved from the dining room back to the main living area where they sat next to each other on the sectional sofa. Camilla crossed her legs and made sure to keep a gap between them, but Hunter closed in, leaving only a minor space between them. He offered Camilla another glass of wine, which she took despite her earlier statement that the previous glass was her last.

"You wouldn't happen to have musical talent, would you?" Hunter asked. He suddenly wanted to know everything about Camilla. She'd been a refreshing change to the women who only came around in the hopes that he would bed them. It didn't matter that Hunter never propositioned the women. They would lay themselves at his feet, and being the bachelor he was, more times than he wanted to admit, he took them up on their offer.

Camilla giggled. "I sure do. I have this splendid rendition of Etta James' 'At Last' that I sing in the shower."

The timbre in which Hunter's laugh trekked from the depths of his throat sent a detonation of chills scouring over Camilla's skin. She joined his chortle, unable to keep from smiling as she watched his gorgeous masculine face spread with a humorous glee.

She shrugged. "I'm just keeping it real. No one can top my shower song. Not even Rihanna herself."

Hunter tried to calm himself, but Camilla kept at it. It had been a long time since he'd laughed that hard about anything, and he couldn't help but appreciate her for it.

"A woman with a sense of humor," he said amid a chuckle. "I love it."

Camilla stood and did a curtsy then pushed off his shoulder playfully.

"I'm just being myself," she said.

Hunter nodded. "I think I love yourself," he said before realizing what he'd actually spoken.

Both of their smiles dropped instantly, and they stared at each other.

"I didn't mean… what I meant was—"

"It's okay," Camilla spoke softly. "I understand what you meant."

Hunter assessed her for another long minute. Camilla had turned him into a stuttering fool. Never mind it had lasted only a second. It was new. She got under his skin, and he didn't know how to feel about that.

Camilla tried to change the subject. "I guess you asking me that question means you have musical talent yourself?"

Going with her flow, Hunter reached for her hand, and Camilla sat back down next to him. Her thigh grazed against his, and she tried to ignore the ripple of heat that poured over her.

"I've got a thing for the saxophone. I play down at the Velvet Café once a week. You should come and check me out."

"Nice," she said, "you have to have solid talent to play that instrument. I don't mean because of its actual sound but because of its build. You need big hands and a bit of muscle just to hold that big boy up." Camilla swept her eyes over Hunter's solid physique. "Which I'm sure you have no problems with," she added with a sip of her wine.

Hunter chuckled. "For someone who doesn't play the instrument, you know enough about it."

Camilla shrugged. "I played around with instruments in college, but it was never my thing. However, I remember staying away from the saxophone specifically because of how large it was."

"It's not so bad once you get used to it. I'd like to show you if you'd be willing to learn a thing or two."

Camilla twisted her lips. "I dunno…"

Hunter chuckled again. "I'll hold it for you, and all you have to do is put your lips on its tip and blow."

A quiver raced down Camilla's spine, and a freak nasty image of her giving Hunter fellatio ripped through her mind. She blinked frantically. *Oh my God*. A nervous laugh skittered from her.

"I'll keep that in mind," she said, hoping to get it out of her head before the night was over.

"Trust me, you'll like it."

Camilla's thoughts were still in the gutter, and she haphazardly licked her lips. *I'm sure*.

"And you know that because you know me," she asked, keeping a neutral expression as she tried to extinguish the naughty reflections.

She was being sarcastic. This much Hunter knew.

"You seem like the type of person who likes to have fun and learn a thing or two. I feel you will enjoy it."

I feel it, too. "Hmm, you might be right," she said, ignoring her thinking. "Okay, on what days do you play?"

"Tuesdays and Wednesdays."

"Tuesday's tomorrow," she said, and Hunter nodded. "What time do you start?"

"Six p.m. I'll save you a seat on the front row, but you don't really need the spot since you won't see me."

Camilla frowned. "What do you mean?"

"I'm not on stage. There's usually a speaker on stage. The club is known for its undiscovered spoken word artists."

"So, you'll be in the background, but the music will be coming from you."

"Yes."

Camilla thought it over. "All right. That would give me a chance to focus on your talent and not your... um," she fumbled, and Hunter's gaze darkened.

"Say what's on your mind, Angel."

Camilla sucked in a breath of wind. "It'll keep me from being distracted is all."

Hunter's eyes fell over her. "Do I distract you?"

A scutter of heat sailed over her. She didn't want to stroke his ego. Camilla knew he'd probably had enough of that to go around for a lifetime. But once again, her fast-talking had her caught in a bind.

"You're a beautiful man, Hunter. I'm sure you distract many women. I apparently don't seem to be immune."

"Why thank you, Angel. I've been called many things, but I don't think beautiful is one of them."

Camilla arched a brow. "Lies."

Hunter smirked. "I don't mean I've never been compli-mented, but beautiful? He rubbed his chin. "Yeah... that's a new one."

"Maybe I see you differently than everyone else. No one is represented the same through someone else's eyes."

"True that." Hunter's hand lifted to her face, and his fingers caressed the skin on her chin. "I think, it is you that is the beautiful one."

Camilla blushed. "Thank you."

"It's been more of a pleasure than you know. Thank you for taking pity on me and allowing me to sit and eat with you this morning."

Camilla's soft smile turned into a smirk. "You're welcome."

The temperature in the room grew warmer, and Camilla dropped her gaze from his to check the time.

"I must get going. I've overstayed my welcome."

She stood and slipped a hand down her blouse and skirt to smooth them down. Hunter rose with her.

"I've enjoyed your company. You haven't overstayed at all. As a matter of fact, I haven't had enough of you."

Camilla squirmed, and she bit the corner of her lip with her teeth.

"Maybe I'll come back sometime."

Instantly, Camilla wanted to rebuke herself. *What the hell, girl?*

Hunter stepped closer to her, the wall of his breastplate grazing across her own. Her eyes dropped, and she inhaled a thorough breath. Reaching out, Hunter trailed a finger up the archway in her neck and tapped the underlay of her chin. Camilla lifted her head, bringing her lips mere seconds from his. Her heart knocked as he moved toward her slowly, his eyes low and breath even.

Camilla froze. When his mouth sank into hers she let go of a breath she wasn't aware she was holding. Their lips mixed; him covering her bottom while hers covered his top. Heat sailed over them in a blanket so warm the fine hairs on Camilla's neck stood at attention. *Oh God.* She panted into his mouth, and their lips shifted as Hunter pulled in her top and she his bottom. A blaze of heat traveled down the middle of her chest to her clitoris, and suddenly Camilla wanted to jump his bones. But when she dispelled the notion, Hunter wrapped his thick arms and muscular biceps around her waist. With a tug, he drew her nearer, and the hardness of his shaft pressed against her belly. *Oh shit.*

Maybe she could have a one-night stand with him. It would be harmless, right? Just enough to get her rocks off and never speak to him again. *But he's your neighbor.* Camilla pulled back with all the strength she could muster, her hand slipping up his arms to stop him. Hunter's simmering gaze tore through her, and again, Camilla's heartbeat raced.

"I should get going," her throaty voice cajoled. She took a step back, effectively removing herself from Hunter's arms. "I need my card back now. Please."

Hunter's tongue traced his lips, and he eyed her to make sure she was okay.

"I can't say that I didn't mean to kiss you because I did," he said. "However, if you feel I was out of line, I do apologize."

"Oh no," Camilla said quickly. "You're fine, I just..." she cleared her throat. "Need to be getting ready for work in the morning is all."

Hunter nodded. "Understood. I'll be right back," he said, stepping away from her reluctantly.

Camilla let go of another extended breath and managed to straighten herself. Hunter's return wasn't as quick as when he'd left to put on a shirt, and Camilla couldn't help but wonder what was taking him so long. She needed to get out of his place before she changed her mind and did something she'd end up regretting. *Don't go back there.* The voice in her head called, just as she thought to go seek him out. But thankfully he rounded the corner and strolled up to her.

"Let me walk you to your apartment."

Camilla's eyes lurched. "Oh no, that's okay."

"I want to make sure you get there safely," he said. "I promise it's not so I can stalk you."

As if I'd mind you stalking me.

"This is supposed to be the safest building in Chicago, I think I'll be all right."

Hunter eyed her for another long moment.

"At least let me walk you to the elevator."

Camilla swallowed. If that's what it took to keep up the charade she had to go with it.

"All right," she said.

They left Hunter's apartment and strolled unhurriedly down the hallway. They stole peeks at each other but kept silent, both mulling over the kiss they'd shared. At the elevator, Hunter hit the button then removed a card and slipped it into Camilla's hand just as the doors dinged.

"Thank you for dinner," she said, moseying leisurely inside the metal box.

"Anytime." His smile was charming, and Camilla blushed then flipped the card around in her hand as she glanced down at it. Without warning, a frown covered her face, and she glanced up.

"Hey, this isn't my card."

It read Amex, Hunter Valentine. On the back a four-digit pin number and a ten-digit phone number were written on a sticky note. Confused, she swept her eye back at him again.

"This way you'll have no choice but to revisit me. Take care… Angel."

And just like that the elevator doors closed, and he was gone.

Chapter Nine

ast night, Camilla paced the lobby for thirty full minutes before returning to her apartment. The entire time she thought of nothing but Hunter. The nice dinner they'd had, the kiss, the card, and the fact that he hadn't even asked how she knew where he lived. Now sitting behind WTZB studio lights, Camilla's mind was still on Hunter, mostly because shortly after arriving at the news station, she'd found out while going through morning reports that Hunter was in the rotation to be interviewed today. A flush of warmth swirled around her face, making her blush instantly. Apparently, after the news cycle the day before, the station received a call from the man himself. According to everyone there, it was a rarity for Hunter or any other celebrity to call in and request an interview.

The team was ecstatic, and of course, he asked specifically for the new face of WTZB to be the one to interview him. Camilla. She fumbled with her earpiece thinking about his sneaky tactics. He'd known yesterday while they had dinner that she would be interviewing him today. So, why hadn't he mentioned it to her? Camilla couldn't get her thoughts together adequately to call him for a practice run. It was enough that she'd tossed and turned last night with wicked foreplay with him in her dreams.

"We're live in 5, 4, 3, 2…"

The light on the camera turned red, and the station's recorded morning introduction sailed across the viewers' televisions before cutting to Gerald Meyer.

"It's a great morning at WTZB, and I'm here with my lovely co-anchor Camilla Augustina. Good morning, folks, and good morning, Camilla."

Camilla's smile spread across her face, and her brown eyes lit up as she acknowledged Gerald. "Good morning, Gerald, and good morning, Chicago. Today's weather is better than yesterday's, I think, or is Chicago's weather normally in this much disarray?"

Gerald laughed a heavy chuckle that brightened his already lively face.

"I'm sorry to say that I think it's always like this."

"Oh boy," Camilla responded.

"You'll get used to it eventually, then when you go back home to Florida, you'll feel like an outsider." Gerald laughed at his own joke.

"Now that's something I can't imagine."

"Well you've lived there all your life, so somethings will never change, but Chicago may grow on you. Our weather is interchangeable, and the environment is healthy."

"Which is why I chose this city to move to, and speaking of the environment," Camilla turned her attention toward the live camera, "today, we're speaking with Hunter Valentine about his green energy initiative and the ribbon-cutting ceremony that will be held later this week."

"Friday," Gerald intervened.

"Yes," Camilla picked up. "Have we been invited to cover it?"

"We're working on it," Gerald cajoled. "Maybe we should ask the man of the hour."

"You're right." Camilla glanced back at the camera. "Mr. Valentine, do we have you on the line?"

Camilla held her breath, and the authoritative voice that was Hunter Valentine crooned through the studio speakers of WTZB.

"Good morning, Camilla," he said, deciding not to be formal with her, live air be damned. "It's nice to hear from you again."

Camilla's grin was uniformed in a concealed covering that presented a beautiful smile but underneath it all, Camilla was completely flushed, and the stinging heat that slipped over her flesh traveled to her nipples. *Oh, dear God.* Not only had Hunter made it known that they were previously acquainted with that introduction, but his baritone voice didn't disappoint. Camilla hoped beyond hope that her now rock-solid areolas weren't protruding through the silk blouse she sat comfortably in.

Damn, I shouldn't have worn this blouse.

Camilla was stuck in her smile, and before anyone had a chance to notice the absence of her response, Hunter moved to Gerald, making sure to acknowledge him as well.

"Good morning, Mr. Meyers, thank you both for taking my call."

Gerald spoke up. "We're your number one fans here at WTZB. I just wish I could've gotten the warm welcome Camilla just received."

Gerald chuckled and so did Hunter, but their voices were entirely different. Where Gerald's was an upbeat guffaw, Hunter's was a deep thunderous chuckle that threatened Camilla's heartbeat.

"I'm just kidding. I know it's reserved for the ladies. I'm not jealous," Gerald continued to joke.

"I wouldn't go so far as to say that," Hunter acquitted.

"No?"

"Nah, just for Ms. Augustina," Hunter replied.

It was as if he were trying to take her down before she could gather herself. Was it possible Hunter didn't know the effect he had on her? She'd told him last night that he could be a bit of a distraction. So, either he didn't care, or he genuinely wasn't aware that he was doing it at that very moment.

Shaking herself inwardly, Camilla put her professional hat on and charged full throttle into the interview. "It is nice to hear from you again, Mr. Valentine." She turned the tables by addressing him formally, and he caught her drift. Although she couldn't see him, Camilla felt entuned with his aura and could immediately tell there was a delicious grin on his strong face.

"We're interested to know how your green energy initiatives project came to fruition. Can you tell us a little bit about it?"

"Certainly," he paused. "Our environment is threatened by the burning of fossil fuels that we as a people release into it daily. Coal, oil, and gas have a harmful effect on not only our airwaves, but the earth in general. If we plan to leave a planet to our children and our children's children, then something must change, and it starts with each individual currently inhabiting this wonderful planet today.

"My contribution to what I like to call the Save the Earth project starts with my green energy initiative. Having the power to make a change with a vast impact is something I take seriously. Because although this is business for me, it's personal, too. Without a clean environment, the human race loses. We have to do better. We must.

I've partnered with Toyota to bring more energy efficient cars to consumers. Vehicles that the everyday citizen can afford and give their own helping hand to our environment by simply exchanging their gas induced vehicles for a better, stronger, much more resourceful automobile. Toyota's Prius is the world's top-selling hybrid electric vehicle on the market. Its aerodynamic features are unmatched to any other hybrid out there. Along with the charging stations provided by my company, the Toyota Prius is a smart innovation that's hard to pass up. And," he paused. "It comes in a variety of colors."

Gerald and Camilla chuckled.

"Tell me, Camilla," Hunter said, "are you driving and energy efficient vehicle?"

"No." Camilla quickly cleared her throat. Her voice had

dipped soft and sultry. "I don't have a car now since I'm new in town, I'm driving a rental."

"Even better." Hunter's deep voice sailed through her earpiece and stroked her flesh. "What's your favorite color, Camilla?"

"I wouldn't say I have a favorite color, but if I had to choose, I'd say salmon pink and apple green."

Those were her sorority colors, and Hunter caught on immediately. A full-on smile trekked across Hunter's lips, and he felt refreshed that she'd chosen to add a piece of their personal conversation into this one.

"Now if you tell me Toyota's got those colors, then I'd run down there myself and signup," Camilla added.

"You should come anyway. Consider this my personal invitation to the ribbon-cutting ceremony. I'd love to show you and WTZB an up-close look at what we've put together."

Camilla cut her eyes quickly at Gerald. She wasn't the reporter for the station, so it wasn't her place to accept his request. Standing behind the cameras, Allison and the station's owner Avery Michele smiled brightly. Avery nodded, as if to say, it's okay to accept. Still Camilla hesitated.

"We would love to be there. Thank you for inviting us," she said after a quick consideration.

"My pleasure. I'll provide transportation for you, Friday at two p.m."

"We'll be ready, and thank you for calling in."

"You're welcome. I'll see you soon." The studio ended the call.

"It looks like we have a date, folks," Gerald shouted.

This time Camilla couldn't hold back her blush. Her brown cheeks darkened, and her smile took Hunter's breath away. Her reaction was beautiful, and he couldn't take his eyes off the screen as he stood in his office.

"Oh, Gerald," Camilla drawled teasingly. "Don't stir up trouble for me now. We all know Mr. Valentine may have a woman at home. She's probably ready to come down to the station and hurt me now," she continued to tease.

Hunter wished he was still on the line to dispel that comment, but he would address it later, if, Camilla decided to still come to Velvet Café and hear him play.

There was a swift knock at his door followed by a feminine voice.

"Nice interview."

Hunter didn't take his eyes from the TV. His assistant was always somewhere lurking when she didn't need to be.

"Thanks. Is everyone in the conference room," he asked.

She cleared her throat. "Let me check on that."

He listened as her soft steps glided away. He shook his head.

Most of the women he'd hired to be his assistant in the past were pretty much the same. It was hard to find good help without the woman being attracted to him. Devin, his right-hand man had warned him about hiring anyone with an X chromosome; spoken like a true chauvinist. Hunter ignored him. He hired according to the experience and attributes a person could add to his company, not because of gender.

Dismissing the thoughts, Hunter watched as Camilla's

luscious lips moved. She'd worn her hair in a bounty of curls different from the straight layered look she'd had the day before. As he stared, Hunter remembered the taste of her mouth, the softness of her lips, and the way he'd wanted desperately to send his tongue on an invading crusade. Camilla probably didn't think so, but Hunter had held back not wanting to come on too strong but needing to connect with her all the same. She took the viewers on a commercial break with promises to come back and hand over the segment to Dan the weatherman.

Hunter stepped to the high definition screen and stretched his long arm out, powering off the electronic. Strolling around his large corner office desk, he removed his suit jacket and tossed it over his arm then bent to retrieve his suitcase. After this meeting, he would leave for the day and head to the flower shop before arriving at Velvet Café. He wanted to make an impression on Camilla, and in the back of his mind, Hunter was still trying to figure out, why.

Chapter Ten

"*I* don't mean to be up in your business but that was about the most exciting live display of flirtation I've seen in my tenure here at WTZB. If you need a friend to talk about it with, I'm your girl."

Camilla tried to suppress her grin, but it was too late. The corners of her lips lifted with ease, and she looked left and right down the hallway before grabbing Allison's hand and trudging into the back newsroom.

Camilla pivoted and shut the door behind them then breathed in a deep breath. Allison looked on with excitement in her eyes, waiting for the juice she was sure their newest co-anchor would deliver.

Instead, Camilla's bubbling expression tanked, and her shoulders slumped. "I honestly don't know."

Allison's forehead crinkled. "Okay…" she said. "Well, what do you know?"

"I met Hunter my first day on the job. Apparently, we live in the same building, and—"

"Wait! You live in the same building?"

"Yeah."

"Girl, you must be loaded to live on the same block as Hunter Valentine!"

Camilla shrugged. "I'm not loaded, but I had a pretty hefty savings before moving to Chicago. Notice the past tense in the word had."

Allison laughed. "I guess you emptied it moving into his building."

"I didn't know I was moving into his building, I just chose a location I felt was in the safest part of town. I mean, if we're realistic, Chicago isn't the best place to move according to safety reports. My parents were against it in the beginning, and I managed to get my dad to come around. That was only after we toured here and found The Regency."

Allison's jaw dropped. "You live in The Regency!?"

Camilla nodded. "I thought you knew that."

"Why would I?"

"Because it's where Hunter lives."

"I never knew where Hunter laid his head. Trust me, if I did, I might try to break in, you know."

Camilla's eyes popped.

"What?" Allison held her hands out then dropped them at her side. "At least I'm being honest."

"Hmmm." Camilla didn't know how to feel about Allison's profound honesty. "What kind of reporter doesn't know where their hometown celebrities live? Surely, you've staked out before or followed him. Even the humblest of reporters do that."

"Because I'm not a reporter. I'm an assignment editor. I don't report the news."

She had a point, Camilla thought. "But you do have a reporter here, right?"

"Of course, and you've just taken her job for what may be one of the biggest in-person interviews at the station this year."

Camilla frowned. "What do you mean?"

"Hunter's invited you specifically to his ribbon-cutting ceremony, and Avery gave the okay."

"Yeah, but he said you and WTZB, so actually that means all of us."

"Wait a minute, are you seriously trying to tell me you didn't catch all of that flirtation?"

Camilla pursed her lips and shifted her weight from one foot to the other.

"I felt it." *Boy, had she felt it.* "But still he did say AND WTZB."

Allison gave a quick wave with her hand and shook her head.

"Yeah, but why do I feel like a piece of this story is missing? So, you met Hunter the first day and what happened?"

"I was eating breakfast, and there were no other seats, so he asked if he could dine with me."

Allison rotated her hand as if to say, "go on."

"And..." Camilla pondered about how much information to divulge. "And, well, we had a good morning. I don't think he's flirtatious on purpose. Like you said yesterday, he's a charming guy, it's easy for one to think he may be interested in them."

"So, this is why you asked so many questions about him at lunch yesterday."

Camilla's brows furrowed. "I didn't ask so many questions about him. We did a segment on him, so I asked normal questions."

"Unhuh, so after this breakfast," Allison interrupted, "did he give you his number, or are you guys dating, or—"

"Whoa, slow down," Camilla said. Allison had her head spinning. If she thought Corinne was an investigator, she was wrong. "You might not be a reporter, but I think you missed your calling."

Allison's lips twitched. "Whatever, girl."

They both chuckled.

"I'm just saying. You ask a million questions a second. I can't keep up."

"I'm so sorry. As I said, I didn't want to get all in your business."

Camilla twisted her lips.

"Okay, maybe just a little, but hey, news like this is something I only dream about. A possible romance brewing between the new anchor and the bachelor of all bachelors, where do I sign up for the live viewing?"

"Oh my God, did anyone ever tell you, you should write a book? That's how dramatic you're being right now."

"Hmm, I don't know. What I do know is if Hunter's got his eyes on you, then you might as well be off the market."

"Hmph, wasn't aware I was a grocery store," Camilla mumbled.

Allison laughed. "That was a good one, but just so you know, I'll probably be nosy from here on out."

At Camilla's lifted brow, Allison added. "Hey, I don't have a love life. I've got to live it through somebody."

"So why haven't you ever dated him then?"

"One doesn't just date Hunter, or his fine ass brothers."

This piqued Camilla's interest.

"What do you know about his brothers?"

"Not much besides the fact they're all gorgeous, millionaire bachelors who own their own businesses, live for the fast life, and keep a gang of women. I mean you never see them without one. A few graduated from Morehouse, but others I believe graduated from Harvard. The middle one, Lance, is the sexiest to me, but he's never in town. I do believe he's a director of some kind, but I can't be too sure. Oh, and Xavier, he's fine, too, honey, whew." She wiped her forehead. "But Xavier stays on the private jet like he lives airborne, I swear."

Camilla tilted her head and folded her arms then muttered. "Not much, huh?"

Allison shut her lips tight and widened her eyes a bit embarrassed at her rambling.

"My bad."

"You're good, girl." Camilla turned to leave and paused. "Oh, I have the money from lunch that I borrowed yesterday." Camilla dug into her pocket and removed the twenty-dollar bill. She didn't want to actually pull money from Hunter's account, but he'd left her no choice. What man would give a woman he didn't know access to his funds anyway? That, Camilla was still confused about.

"Keep the change." Camilla made a note to self to pay Hunter back.

"Are you sure?" Allison said, tucking the bill inside her own pocket.

Camilla chuckled. "Yeah, you're good. So, are you game for going with me to the ribbon-cutting ceremony then?"

Allison thought it over. "I remember him specifically asking you."

"We've been over this."

"Okay, fine, I'll go with you since you're scared to be with him alone," Allison teased. "But trust me, once I'm there, you'll wish you were."

"I highly doubt it."

"Highly?"

"Hunter's attractive and suave, but I've had enough of men to last a lifetime."

"Sounds like a broken heart and an ex that you could strangle."

"I'm over it, but I'm not looking to get caught up in whatever game Mr. Valentine is playing. I want no parts of it."

Even as the words left Camilla's lips, she didn't believe them. Deep down, Camilla looked forward to hearing him play at the Velvet Café even though she continued to tell herself it was just his music that interested her.

"Unhuh, okay." Allison didn't believe her either. "Lunch?"

"As long as you don't ask another question about Hunter."

"Fine, have it your way."

The women strolled to the door, and as an afterthought, Camilla asked, "Do you know if he has a brother named Trevor?"

Allison turned with a hand on her hip. "If I can't talk about him, then neither can you."

"All right, all right," Camilla repeated.

"But no, not that I know of."

"Hmmm," was all she said.

Why Hunter Valentine fascinated her was beyond Camilla, but she lied to herself once again, saying it wasn't in her interest to find out. Before they could make it out of the building, Allison and Camilla ran into a delivery coming through the door.

"Camilla Augustina," the guy asked.

Both Camilla and Allison paused and stared at each other with invested interest.

"That's me," Camilla spoke up.

"These are for you."

He handed her a bouquet of long stem salmon pink and apple green roses. They were in a black square box with gold lettering, and immediately Camilla knew they were from Hunter. He intentionally used both of their pledge colors, leaving no room for Camilla to think they were from someone else.

A broad smile crossed Allison's face, and her mouth parted in a widespread grin. "Those are beautiful," she said.

But all Camilla could do was stare at the gorgeous flowers and remind herself to breathe so she wouldn't get too excited. But she was already too excited; her heart rocked in her chest, and her nerves tingled her flesh. It wasn't the first time she'd received flowers, but it was the first time anyone had put so much thought into the gift. How sexy of him. Without trying she smiled, soft and slow.

Glancing over at Allison, she spoke, "I'm going to put these in my office if you don't mind waiting another few minutes."

Allison shook her head. "I don't mind at all."

Without another word, Camilla turned, and in a daze, trailed back down the hallway. Once she entered her office, Camilla shut the door and dropped her handbag. Leaning against the wooden frame, she stuffed her nose in the bouquet, and it set off an array of sweet fragrances. Her mind wandered to the last thought she'd had about it not being in her interest to find out what Hunter was up to.

But maybe, just maybe, she might.

Chapter Eleven

*J*t was the last thing Camilla expected to see when she sashayed through the doors of the Velvet Café. The dim lighting cast a red glow across the club. At some tables, a hookah sat on top as women and men pulled from its prongs. Her eyes trailed around the room, taking in some Rastafari looking men with dreads that hung down their back, full beards, and brown skin. Smoke from the hookah poured from their nostrils; they were casual in jeans and a simple T-shirt.

Even the women appeared to be dressed casually, and it made Camilla wonder if she was overdressed. She glanced down at herself, and the first thing she saw was cleavage. The body-hugging, knee-length black dress stretched her bodacious form like a soft wave. The three-inch open toe heels gave just a peek of her feet, and black see-through pantyhose shaped her legs. Camilla cleared her throat and tugged at the bottom of the short jacket that stopped just below her breasts. She'd only worn it to cover her arms since the winter season was still full on blast.

"Good evening," A woman strolled up to her, wearing an apron and a uniform shirt holding the Velvet Café's logo.

"Good evening," Camilla responded.

"First time here?"

"Is it that obvious?"

The woman smiled and held her hand out for a shake.

"I'm Dee-Dee. I'll take care of you tonight, no worries. Are you alone?"

Camilla opened her mouth to speak, but she didn't know if she should say she was there to hear Hunter play or not.

"She's with me," a nocturnal voice pronounced.

A shiver slipped down Camilla's skin as she turned around to face Hunter. He towered over her, large and in charge, wearing a button-down shirt with a loose tie and the first button undone. Camilla's eyes ran the length of his masculine throat, to his strong chin and tempting lips. She couldn't help herself. Camilla's eyes hovered on his mouth before running up his manly nose, to his smoldering eyes. *Jesus, help me, Lord.* Camilla had never seen a man so fine. It was ridiculous. She smiled delightedly and took note of his rolled-up sleeves and the prickly hairs on his forearm with hands that rested inside his pockets.

Camilla felt lulled toward him, and as if she'd moved, the minor space between them was closed, but it was Hunter who sealed it.

"Thank you for coming," his deep voice beat.

A blush reddened her sienna cheeks. "Well, after you

practically begged me to come, I guess I had no choice," she teased.

Hunter's dark gaze lightened, and his lips spread into a smirk of a smile.

"If that's what it takes to get you here, then so be it."

Camilla chuckled. "I was just kidding."

"I wasn't."

The flush on her face remained as her cheeks tightened at his insinuation. She studied him as his gaze poured over her, encased in a dominant proclamation. The virile announcement was loaded with branding, and anyone looking on would swear they belonged to one another; except everyone knew Hunter Valentine. He'd been single for as long as single had been a part of the dictionary. And until he made it known otherwise, they would expect that Camilla was someone he was after for merely the chase of it.

That thought wasn't far away from Camilla's mind either. Which is why she couldn't let this little thing that seemed to be going on between them get up under her skin. *Remember the three females that left his apartment.* How could she forget? Her mind wouldn't let her. *Besides that, Steven.* Thinking about Steven just made her want to regurgitate her lunch, but it got her right together.

"Sorry about the smoke," Hunter said, penetrating her thoughts.

Camilla glanced around again. "It's not so bad, I guess. I mean, it isn't real smoke. Smells kind of like candy."

Hunter chuckled. "Do you smoke?"

"No," Camilla said quickly. "Do you?"

Hunter eyed her. "Would it bother you if I did?"

Camilla folded her arms, draping them across her heavy breasts. The strain her limbs caused on her chest made the peek of cleavage practically burst from the opening. Hunter's gaze traveled down her flesh over the roundness of her bosom. His dick bounced, and inwardly, he cautioned himself. *Down, boy.*

"If I'm to be honest, then yes, it would bother me."

Hunter raised a brow. "Why?"

"Because smoking is bad for your health. Surely you've seen the cigarette commercials where they—"

"I didn't know you cared about my health, Angel…"

Camilla's words were caught in her throat. She closed her mouth, then licked her lips, while they held each other's stares.

"I mean," Camilla sighed. She'd only known Hunter for not even seventy-two hours, but what would be the purpose of denying what he said when it was the truth. "Oddly, Mr. Valentine, I do." She grabbed the knot in his tie and curled her fingers around it, then pulled slightly, turning her face up. Leaning into him, she spoke, "Do you have a problem with that?"

Hunter's hands left his pockets and found their way around Camilla's waist. He drew her so close their heart-beats matched, and their breathing became one. The shift happened so suddenly that Camilla was coupled in his arms before she had a moment to blink, think, or speak her next words. His head leaned closer to hers, and the tips of their noses touched when he spoke.

"I find it equally strange that I, too, care about your well-being, Angel. Almost as if there is an eternal connection that links us." His hands roamed up her back, leaving a trail of spiraling heat encompassing her skin. "And for the record, I don't smoke. I was just yanking your chain."

A delectable smile covered Camilla's face. She felt foolish. He'd baited her, and she'd fallen for it hook, line, and sinker. It made her wonder if he was a man of many games, so she asked.

"Do you get off on playing with a woman's mind, Mr. Valentine?"

His brows furrowed. "That wasn't my intention."

"Oh?"

He pulled back slightly. "No, I simply wanted to know if you care."

"By playing games and pretending you smoke when you don't. That's deceitful." She put some stank in her attitude.

Hunter drew back more. "Deceitful? You're taking it the wrong way. I was merely trying to—"

Camilla's laugh cut into Hunter's explanation. He eyed her curiously then nodded with slow understanding.

"You're messing with me," he said, stating the obvious.

Camilla laughed harder. "Man, you were like, no – um, I," she mimicked stuttering and motioning with her hands.

Hunter dropped back down to eye level with her, and as she laughed his thick fingers danced at her sides, tickling her sensitive skin through the thin fabric of her dress. Her laugh picked up, and she fell over in Hunter's arms. He enjoyed the spread of her mouth and lighting of her face. She smelled of warm vanilla and jasmine, and her skin was soft to the touch. Without pause, he nuzzled his nose between her neck and chin, inhaling her natural sweet scent. It tickled his nostrils, making them flare and sending a buzz feed over his skin.

Camilla jumped quickly away from him and held out her hands to stop his attack. "Hey!"

"Oh, you've started, now you can't finish, huh?"

"I was just giving you a taste of your own medicine."

"Is that what you were doing?"

"Yes!" She said as he broke through her barrier to stand right in front of her. Camilla's hands slipped up his chest, and her butt bumped into the bar. "Ah!" she squealed with a turn to find out what was behind her.

The patrons sitting alongside glanced at them then went back to their drinks. The bartender held a smile as he watched them much like some of the others in the room.

"Mr. Valentine, can I get you and your lady friend here a drink?"

Hunter kept his gaze on Camilla. "Would you like something to drink, Angel?"

"I could use a little something. What would you suggest?"

"You may like their Between the Sheets cocktail, but they also make a killer margarita."

"And what will you have," she asked.

"I'm up next, so I'll chill until my set is over."

"Oh."

"If you get lonely, don't fret, I'll be back before you miss me."

Camilla put on her sister girl voice again and braced her hands against her thick hips. "I'd have to like you to miss you."

Hunter released her and planted his hands on both sides of the bar, locking her in as he leaned toward her lips. "I was hoping by now you might," his thick voice drummed.

Camilla ignored the turbulence of her nerves and kept up her pretense.

"I've only known you," she snapped her fingers, "that long, why would I like you so suddenly?"

Hunter's tongue traveled across his teeth, and he sucked air between them. "Because I like you. And when you know, you know."

Camilla's eyes faltered to his lips, and another quiver ran the course of her body. "You don't even know me," she said, her voice dropping the sister girl tone and driving into a sultry one. "What could you possibly like?"

Hunter didn't have to think long. He answered that question right away.

"You go after what you want in life. Letting nothing hold you back. You uprooted your way of living in Florida, the only life you've known and took a chance on your elevation by moving here. I'm sure you had doubts about possible failure, but you didn't let that deter your decision." He paused, and his stare roamed over her face. "You uplift your sisters. They're no blood relation to you and yet you love them all the same. Your sole reason for joining Alpha Kappa Alpha derived from wanting to uplift. That makes you beautiful inside and out."

He paused once more and removed one hand from the bar to trail his fingers alongside her neck and chin. "Besides those things, your face lights up when you smile. Bright enough to alleviate a dark room. You're silly, playful, and a pleasure to be around. That makes me like you, Angel, more than I probably should."

Hunter glanced over at the bartender. "She'll have a skinny margarita." His eyes fell back to Camilla. "I want to start her off with something that will go down warm and slow. I wouldn't want to overwhelm her with something so strong on her first try."

Camilla swallowed, and she wondered if he was speaking about something else entirely. Damn, she wanted to kiss him. His lips were so painstakingly close that it struck a nerve not to. The fact was Camilla liked him, too, but God, it couldn't be this easy, could it? No man on this earth had ever wooed her like Hunter. But here she was fighting the temptation to stick out her tongue and lick his mouth. A glass slid down the bar, and Hunter caught it in his palm.

"Merci," he said, thanking the bartender in French.

Hunter handed the glass over to Camilla, and she took a long hard sip, one that gave her courage. She moved within the cocoon of his sheltered position and twirled around, sticking a hip out.

Tossing a glance over her shoulder, she crooned, "You didn't say anything about liking my physical attributes."

Hunter's simmering stare darkened, and he took a bold step toward her. His pelvis grazed her derriere as his hands slipped down her waist and covered her hips. He felt her quiver and her body torched to the heat of his palms. She was so soft that his fingers could melt into her; so, they did, digging at her curvy hips. Leaning closer, Hunter pulled her, giving her buttocks a grinding bounce into his front.

When the lights dimmed further, Hunter cursed. He

knew that was his cue to get backstage. And just as he'd thought about capturing Camilla's mouth, he heard the soft-spoken voice of the owner on stage.

"Good evening," she crooned.

Hunter rotated Camilla around to face him. "I've got to head back." His voice was detrimentally dark. "But I'll return to finish this." Hunter pulled her face toward his and kissed her lips hotly then released her before she could take in a complete breath.

She watched him stride purposefully away and imagined what the magnificence of his ass looked like underneath his pants. A riot of chills swirled around Camilla as she thought about the brick pressed tightly against her ample bottom. *Damn.* Hunter had her hot and bothered. She took another swig of her skinny margarita. As the vibrating sound of a saxophone surrounded the room, Camilla's phone also rang. She removed the clutch under her arm and opened it to fish around. When her hand grasped it, Camilla retrieved the phone and answered it without looking at the screen.

"Hello."

"Well hello, I'm calling to speak with Camilla Augustina. Is she there?"

Camilla smirked at her friend Corinne. "Ha, ha, very funny."

"Oh, so this is Camilla. Hmmm, I couldn't tell by the throaty bedroom voice. You know we've never had phone sex before, so I just needed to make sure I had the right number."

Camilla rolled her eyes. "Here you go."

"So, who's the voice for, Steven?"

Camilla frowned. "Can you give me a little more credit than that?"

"I would if my best friend didn't keep secrets from me. Nowadays, I don't know what's going on. I guess now that you've moved on, I need to look for another friend. Such a travesty."

"Pouring the theatrics on a little thick, aren't you?"

"No."

Camilla sighed. "Okay, what secrets are you talking about," she asked as the overtone of the saxophone scurried down her spine. *Damn, he was good.*

"First of all, are you in the car or something, what's that music in the background?"

"I'm at a club."

"Going to the club without me. You there with your new bestie?"

"If I didn't know any better, I'd think we were sleeping together the way you sound. And secondly, how am I not supposed to go to the club with you when we live in two different cities?"

Corinne paused. "I guess you've made your point."

Camilla rolled her eyes. "Sometimes, I never know what to expect from you."

"Ha! I could say the same for you. So, if the sexy voice isn't for Steven, then it must be for your new boyfriend."

"Excuse me?"

"The one flirting with you on national television."

"National television? Corinne, what are you talking about?"

"The almighty Hunter Valentine. I saw your news segment. As did everyone else in the country."

Camilla's mouth dropped then closed. "What do you mean everyone else in the country?"

"You actually sound surprised. Honey, you know Hunter is a worldwide sensation, don't you? Doing a story on him is one thing but a live interview is another completely. Your segment is running the airwaves practically on repeat. The whole United States of America is waiting to see your live broadcast at the ribbon-cutting ceremony. To be fair, half of the population is excited about his partnership with Toyota and the charging stations he's implementing. They're already calling him the environmentalist." Corinne chuckled. "The other half though," Corinne whistled, "just want another chance at seeing his gorgeousness on their TV screen."

Camilla was speechless. Her segments at her news station in Florida rarely made national headlines if at all.

"Congratulations, you're a celebrity anchor now. Don't be surprised when you start getting calls from all the top names in news asking you to join their team."

Still Camilla was flabbergasted as Corinne's revelations soared through her mind.

"Now answer my question. Is that voice for Hunter?"

Chapter Twelve

The dynamic range of the saxophone elevated, pulling Camilla's attention. Transfixed, Camilla tuned Corinne out as the frequency serenaded her eardrums. The cluster of vibrations wrapped around her, comforting her soul on a spiritual level. She swayed unknowingly as her body responded to the perfect notes and balance of the instrument. Hunter really knew what he was doing, and Camilla wondered if she could get an encore privately.

Her eyes snapped open. It was then that Camilla even realized she'd closed them. The music lured her, speaking to her psyche so easily that she'd removed herself from the chair and slow danced alone. The phone was in her hand, and her arms wrapped around her body. Even Camilla's thoughts had ventured off, and now she was wondering if she were in control of herself at all.

"Hello!" Corinne screeched from the handset in her palm. "Camilla!?"

Camilla pulled the phone back to her ear. "Yeah, I'm here," she said.

"Girl, I have been calling your name for five full minutes! What happened?"

When Camilla spoke, her voice was straightforward and disoriented.

"I'm surprised you hadn't hung up then."

"I was about to, but I could still hear the music in the background, so I knew the phone was connected. Girl, talk to me, are you all right?"

"Yeah." Camilla stared at the stage, as if waiting for Hunter to appear from behind the curtain. "I'm fine."

"So, what just happened?"

"Something caught my attention. My bad."

Corinne became quiet.

"Listen, I'll call you back, Corinne."

"Wait, are we still having a girl's weekend or what? At least answer that question since I can't seem to get any others answered."

"Um, yeah, sure."

"You don't sound so sure. When you call me back, I'll ask again. But if you take too long, I'm calling you."

"Yes, Mother Dearest," Camilla said sarcastically.

"Mmhmm, bye."

Corinne disconnected the call, and Camilla dropped the phone inside her handbag. Instead of reclaiming her seat, she grabbed her clutch and strolled to the bar.

"What can I get you?" the bartender asked.

"Bathroom?"

"Straight past those tables to the left. There's a short hallway, ladies' room is on your right."

"Thanks."

Camilla sauntered through the tables, catching the eye of every man she passed. Her focus couldn't pay them any mind since the thing she needed most right then was some clarity. As she pushed through the double doors of the ladies' room, Camilla sighed and strolled up to the sink. She dropped her clutch on the counter and turned the faucet on, slipping her hands under the monsoon of chilly water. Bending over, she sent a cold splash of water over her face then grabbed a paper towel and blotted it dry. Since she only wore light foundation, the rinse didn't do much to change her appearance, but being cautious, Camilla reapplied the foundation and added a coat of her Burberry lipstick.

"Get it together, girl," she spoke to herself.

Taking another long look at the image, Camilla reclaimed her clutch and left the ladies' room. The music had taken a different turn as Rihanna's voice now filled the speakers. Camilla took her eyes over the place and spotted Hunter standing near a separate bar in the furthest corner of the room. In front of him, a female with long caramel legs and high heels stood. Her baby doll dress was nowhere near her knees. Camilla paused at the bar next to her and slipped her derriere onto one of the stools in front of it.

"Would you like another skinny margarita," the bartender asked.

Camilla took her gaze back to Hunter and the woman,

unsure if she needed the light mixed drink or something heavy.

"Yes, please," she responded, taking her attention to the bartender.

"Coming right up."

"Thanks."

Camilla glanced back at them and found Hunter laughing out loud. His charming features were elevated, and he shook his head as if whatever the woman said made his day. The woman turned slightly, with a smile also covering her face. Camilla's eyes passed the woman's hair that draped over her shoulders to the middle of her back and she zoomed in on her side profile. She was the same woman Camilla had seen leaving his apartment with two other women. She was the one who had told him she'd be waiting. Knowing this sent a knot of jealousy through Camilla. It was odd since Camilla had no right to be invidious.

But still, she envied the woman and decided it was time for her to go. The bartender returned with the skinny margarita, and Camilla chugged it; tossed it back like it were a mere shot of liquor. She half-slammed the glass down then stood to her feet and was caught up in a dizzy spell. Her hands shot out to the bar as she held herself steady.

"Easy," the bartender said. "Maybe you should sit back down for a second."

He was probably right, Camilla thought, but she didn't want to sit. Her mission was to make it out of the bar before anyone noticed. She stood still for a long moment, holding on to the bar, trying to clear the buzz she'd created. When an overlay of heat passed down her skin, Camilla knew Hunter was there.

"Is everything all right," his deep voice drummed.

Camilla took in a quick breath. "Everything's fine. I was just leaving," she said.

"So soon?" Hunter eyed her, noticing the grip she held on the edge of the bar.

"It's getting late."

Hunter glanced at his Rolex. "It's only nine."

"And I have work in the morning," she said, her voice elevating.

Hunter studied her a little while longer. "If I've done anything to offend you..."

"Why would you think that, Hunter?"

He moved into her space, so close his thigh bumped into hers. The light tap sent a fluttering through her libido, and Camilla silently cursed herself for being so damn out of control with him.

"I'm not sure. You tell me, Angel."

Camilla removed her outstretched hand from the bar and folded her arms across her chest.

"Tell me something, did you know last night while we had dinner that I'd be interviewing you today?"

Hunter's swept a keen eye over her face. "Yes."

"Why didn't you tell me?"

"I didn't know how you'd feel about it."

"Did you think I'd refuse to interview you?"

"I knew there might have been a chance of that. And when I have my mind set on a certain outcome, I don't gamble with it."

Camilla paused, and her eyes roamed over the thick pillar of his throat. "What outcome would that be?"

His stare simmered as it held steady on her. "Getting to know you better?"

"Hmmm. Don't you have enough women to get to know?" Camilla purposefully glanced at the woman he'd just been talking to, causing Hunter to also glance her way.

The woman smiled flirtatiously and winked as she held up a martini glass. Hunter grimaced inwardly. The night he'd taken Kelly, the woman in question, back to his place with her friends, Hunter's gut instinct had been opposed to it originally. But he'd ignored that warning, thinking it wouldn't hurt him in the long run, and here it was biting him in the ass.

"It's not what you think."

"No?"

"No."

"What I think is a few minutes ago you were talking as if you'd like to get to know me, and maybe it's my bed you'd like to get to know." Camilla shrugged. "But I'm not looking for a one-night stand, Mr. Valentine." She looked back at the woman. "Have a good night."

Camilla side-stepped him and put on the best show she could to walk in a straight line. "Damn that skinny margarita," she cursed after making it outside to her car. If she couldn't handle the supposedly light drink, it's a good thing she didn't try the Between the Sheets cocktail.

Plopping down in the driver seat, Camilla turned on the Toyota Camry and sat for a second with her eyes closed and her head against the headrest.

"Now, how are you going to come down here and actually have the nerve to fall in like with Hunter Valentine of all men? How, Camilla?" She chastised herself and waited for the buzz to wear off. When she felt safe to drive, Camilla reopened her eyes just as a soft knock rapped against the window. Carrying her gaze toward the sound, Camilla was met with Hunter's tender stare.

She powered the window down. "Yes?"

"Let me drive you home."

"That's not necessary."

"It may not be necessary, but it's safer."

"Why, Mr. Valentine, are you saying you care about whether I'm safe or not?"

Hunter smirked. "I do. But you already know that, Camilla."

When he used her name, it cleared all necessary tension between them. He'd spoken it as if to let her know that he was serious. Slowly, Camilla dropped her eyes from his, and a small light chuckle escaped her. Whatever it was they were doing was like a cat and mouse game. But the thing that tripped her out was she couldn't stop herself from wanting to play.

With a roll of her eyes, Camilla spoke. "Oh, for goodness' sake, I only had one, maybe two," she paused and questioned her statement, "Two? Three? Oh hell, I only had a few. I'm not drunk. If I were, I wouldn't be in the driver seat. How irresponsible do you think I am?"

She was only toying with him because Hunter got up under her skin.

"Give me your phone number," he said.

Camilla lifted a brow, and Hunter removed his phone from his pocket and slipped it through the window where it fell into her lap. He didn't ask again, only waited for her to do what he requested. They stared each other off, then Camilla found herself lifting the device and swiping the screen.

"It's locked," she said, unamused.

He rambled off the code, and she punched it in, opening the phone. Clearing her throat, Camilla glanced back at him then entered her number and name. When she handed it back, it came with an excuse.

"I only did that because I still have your card, and at some point, you'll get tired of me spending all your money. Then maybe you can release mine."

"I doubt that."

Camilla arched a brow. "You doubt what?"

"That you could spend all my money."

Camilla eyed him. "I could think of a few things to buy. Then you'll change that tune."

Hunter's grizzly laugh tickled Camilla's skin.

"Whatever you say." He rubbed his thick lips together. "I'll make a deal with you?"

Camilla waited for him to proceed.

"Don't pull out of the parking lot until you're absolutely sure you can drive, and I won't bully you about taking you home."

Camilla teased him. "I knew you were a bully."

"Yeah... but not in the way you think, love."

A pocket of heat dissolved between her thighs.

"I'll call you to make sure you got home safely."

Camilla nodded, not trusting her voice.

Hunter nodded once and walked away. She followed him as he reentered the Velvet Café.

Closing her eyes again, Camilla's head fell back, and she rested there for another thirty minutes before finally pulling away from the club.

Chapter Thirteen

*H*unter couldn't keep his mind off her, no matter how hard he tried. He closed the MacBook and sat against his leather office chair. Loosening his tie, Hunter cleared his throat. It had been two days since seeing Camilla at the Velvet Café, and it had been harder than usual for Hunter to erase her from his thoughts. Never mind that he flipped to the morning news every sunrise like clockwork just to get a glimpse of her beautiful face, but he'd set the alarm with his bank to send him a notification whenever a purchase was made, which so far, from what he could tell, was coffee or lunch.

Since departing on fairly odd terms, the conversations on rotation in Hunter's head was much the same. Camilla saw him speaking to Kelly in the club. She insinuated that he had enough women to go around, in so many words. And Camilla wasn't that far off the mark. There wasn't a need to pursue her. Camilla was just another pretty face. Wasn't she? Hunter let out a deep breath. If that was the case, why was he having such a tough time focusing on anything other than her?

He grimaced then chuckled to himself. The last time he'd found himself truly interested in a woman was... was... "Shit," he said, unable to conjure such an instance. Now, not only couldn't he understand why he wanted to make all her dreams come true, but today, he would get to see her face-to-face at the ribbon-cutting ceremony, and then trying to get her out of his head would become even trickier. Hunter glanced at the clock on the wall. 10:32 a.m. He reached for the remote to see if Camilla's segment was still on. Usually, she would be on for an hour and that ended at 10 a.m. But just to be sure, he flipped to WTZB.

You're acting like a sprung puppy, Hunter.

He tried to dismiss the thought, but it taunted him, sending a frustrated vein springing forth on his head. Deciding to go a different route, Hunter shut off the TV and tossed the remote on the surface of his mahogany desk. Standing to his feet, he removed his suit jacket and tossed it over his arm then lifted his suitcase and strolled to the door.

As he approached, a swift knock hit the center of the frame. Hunter reached for the handle and swung it open.

"Delivery for Mr. Hunter Valentine."

Hunter's brows furrowed but that frown quickly dissipated when his gaze dropped down to the salmon pink and apple green box. A broad smile covered his face, and a deep-throated chortle bellowed from him.

"Mr. Valentine," the delivery man asked, making sure Hunter hadn't lost his mind.

Hunter nodded. "That would be me," he said.

The delivery man handed over the box and a card sat on top of it.

"Thank you," Hunter said.

"Have a good day."

Hunter turned back to his desk with the grin still taped across his face. He sat the box down and lifted the top. Beautiful black and gold roses sat inside in a perfect bloom, carrying a fragrance he recognized. Hers. The present thrilled him and gave him pause at the same time. He'd been given phone numbers, addresses, even panties before, but never roses. Especially in this manner. He loved it; her sense of humor, her appreciation of the little things. Without opening the note, he knew that this was her way of saying she was in like with him, too. That made Hunter wonder if she'd been having a hard time getting him off her mind.

Lifting the note, he tapped the edges on the top of his desk a few times while still in awe, and thought, staring down at the gorgeous flowers. He flipped it over in his hand a few times then opened the envelope.

"Thank you for the roses. I didn't forget. I hope you enjoy these as much as I enjoyed mine. Oh, and they didn't cost you too much. I'll pay you back whenever you release my credit card." – Camilla

Another round of rambunctious laughter cruised from him. And to think, he never received a notification that she'd purchased the roses. He sat the roses on the corner of his desk then turned and left the room.

"Leaving early?" His assistant asked.

"Headed downtown. I'll work from there. If any important calls come in, send them to my cell."

"Yes, sir," she said.

Hunter left the building without being stopped again. He was downtown at Millennium Park in record time. He found a parking spot then left the confines of his car. The place was abuzz with activity as representatives from Toyota milled about with representatives from VFC Energy. As Hunter approached, a grin tapered across his lips. A huge deep cherry red bow was laced around three separate charging stations. Each station could charge two energy efficient vehicles at a time.

The new, off-the-showroom-floor Toyota Prius blocked the charging stations to the left and right. The middle charging station was unobstructed since it would be the ribbon Hunter cut to officially open the stations for use. Refreshments and hors d'oeuvres sat on a few tables scattered about, and a single balloon hung from the window on the driver side of each Prius. Local news was already gathered, and Hunter scanned the area for WTZB.

A representative from Toyota approached him. "Excuse me, sir, would you like something to drink?"

"No, thank you. Do you know if anyone has spoken with the camera crews setting up?"

"I don't believe anyone has yet, sir. My boss may speak to them, or he may leave it up to you since you're the face of this campaign."

"We're letting WTZB get the exclusive today, so the

others will have to record from the background," Hunter said.

"Yes, sir."

"Do you know if anyone from the station has arrived?"

The representative looked confused.

"WTZB," Hunter added.

"Oh!" The young man laughed. "Duh, right." He chuckled. "I haven't seen anyone from that station yet, but its' still early. The ceremony doesn't start until two. It's eleven-thirty now."

"Gotcha."

"Sure thing."

The representative turned around and went back to work while Hunter mixed and mingled with other helpers, making sure everything was as it should be. Chicago's weather today held a light breeze. With the way it had been freezing most days and snowing others, it was oddly comforting with the sun shining high and only a wisp of current in the atmosphere. As Hunter worked, his cell phone chimed 2Pac's "Dear Momma" tune, letting him know instantly that his mother Bridgette Valentine was calling.

"Excuse me for a minute," he said to the representative working alongside him.

"How's my favorite lady," he answered.

"Hey baby, I'm doing just fine since the last time we spoke a few days ago. Today's the big day, right? How is everything going down there at the park?"

Hunter swept his eye around with an appreciative gleam in his eye.

"Seems to be going just fine."

"That's good to hear. You always know how to put on a show that's for sure."

Hunter chuckled. "What are you talking about, Mom?"

"You know. I heard that interview you did with that new lady at WTZB. So, did your father. I think I know you well enough to know when my son has taken a liking to someone."

Hunter shut his eyes and kept his grin. "What makes you think I like her? I was simply having a conversation with her about today's event."

"And doing a whole lot of flirting in the process."

"It was harmless. Besides, what makes you think I don't flirt with all the ladies that way? I'm the quintessential bachelor of the year, according to who you ask at the time, anyway."

"I don't need to ask anybody. I'm your mother. Those others are just smitten with you because you're charming, but this girl, Camilla Augustina, she seems to pique your interest."

"Ma, you can tell all of that from the interview?"

"Do I need to answer that, or is it rhetorical, son?"

Hunter laughed out loud, wide and open-mouthed. With his eyes closed, he let the mirth tickle him a bit more before reopening them, but that came with an angelic sight. Camilla stood a few feet in front of him, dressed down in a pinstripe feminine pants suit that hugged her curves in all the right places. Her back was to him as she spoke with a cameraman and another woman from WTZB, but Hunter would never forget the bend in her hips or the arch in her back.

"Maybe just a little," he responded to his mother. "But I hardly know her, so don't get excited."

"Babies!" his mother shouted with a loud chuckle, and Hunter groaned. Bridgette Valentine wanted grandchildren more than his father, and with Hunter being the oldest, he was pressured more about it than his brothers. At least that's how he felt.

He took his eyes off Camilla, knowing he couldn't focus on the conversation with his mother if he continued to stare. Turning to the side, Hunter slipped a hand inside his pocket while the other held the phone to his ear.

"I told you not to get excited."

"I know, I know," she repeated. "Now listen to me. I'm old school, and I'm a Christian, so don't judge me for what I'm about to say."

"Oh no," he said.

"Shush, let me finish." Bridgette paused. "Now I know when you and your brothers moved out of the house, you all had to sow your wild oats before settling down. But, honey, you're thirty-eight now. Forty is right around the corner, and I won't even talk about my age." She huffed. "What I'm trying to say is you better have me a grandchild soon, or… or…"

Hunter raised a brow. "Or what, Ma?"

"Or find you an egg donor and get a surrogate."

Hunter's mouth dropped then closed immediately. Surely his sixty-year-old Christian mother didn't just tell him to find an egg donor.

"I can hear you judging me," Bridgette said.

"How when I haven't said anything?"

"I can hear it."

Hunter let out a breath. "Ma, wouldn't you rather I be married so your grandkids can have a mother?"

"Of course, I would. But I don't have all day for you to get serious with someone. Now, I have a few lady friends who would agree to be your egg donor for a small fee."

"Ma, I hear you, but I've got to go."

Bridgette became quiet. "Are you trying to rush me off the phone, or do you really need to go?"

"I'm not trying to rush you at all. The place is getting crowded." He flipped his wrist and checked the time. "I have about forty minutes before we're live."

Bridgette sighed. "Well, all right. Call me back. This is something pressing on my heart, Hunter."

"Ma, you gotta chill out. I promise not to take too much longer to give you grandkids, okay?"

Bridgette quieted down.

"Ma?"

"Okay. I love you, son."

"I love you, too."

"Talk to you soon."

"Goodbye, Mom."

Hunter ended the call and stood there silent for a minute. His mother had never been that upfront before, but she wasn't alone in her musings. Hunter wanted kids, too. He tossed it around his head for another few seconds when someone cleared their throat.

"Excuse me, Mr. Valentine, are you busy?"

Chapter Fourteen

$\mathcal{H}$unter spun around slowly when he heard her voice. Camilla stood before him with a microphone in hand and a pair of shades on her face. Her hair was in another conglomerate of curls that bounced over her shoulders disappearing behind her back. Her brown skin looked so rich he was sure she'd been dipped in an oven of chocolate. Hunter's eyes traveled to her lips that held a smooth shine. He unknowingly took his tongue across his own, remembering the way she'd tasted.

The blouse that hid her from him was a white ruffled buttoned down, and as the wind current sailed their way, with it was her tantalizing fragrance.

"I'm never too busy for you," he said.

Camilla arched a single brow. She hadn't been expecting that response. A smile covered her lips. "Are you always this charming with the ladies, Mr. Valentine?"

"I think you've asked me that before."

"Oh? And what was your response?"

"Something along the lines of no, only you."

A whimsical laugh tuned from her lips, causing a ring of heat to circle Hunter's skin. "You have a beautiful laugh."

She blushed. "Thank you." Camilla cleared her throat. "So where should we set up? I want to make sure I get the shot I need while not blocking the view of the other stations."

"Don't worry about them. It doesn't matter where you're standing, a good reporter will get their shot if they're on the top of a mountain."

Camilla's melodic laugh cruised from her mouth again, and this time warmth traveled to Hunter's shaft.

"Let me take you out, Camilla."

Although it was cloaked in a request, it wasn't really. Camilla tried not to be surprised by it although she was slightly taken aback.

"I know a place where we can have a little fun and get to know one another."

A riveting swirl of chills scurried across her skin.

"What did you have in mind," she asked.

"It's a surprise, this Saturday."

"Tomorrow?"

"Yes, is that a problem?"

"Um, no, well..." she hesitated. "My close friend from Florida is coming down this weekend. We're supposed to have a girls' night out."

"She misses you already," Hunter asserted. "I can understand that."

"How? I've only literally lived in Chicago a week and a half if that."

"Believe it or not, Angel, it only takes being without you for a few minutes to want you there again."

Camilla was stunned speechless. She genuinely didn't know what to say.

"She can come along, too, if she's up for a double date. I have someone in mind. What's her name?"

"Corinne Thomas. We worked together back in Florida, but she's a flight attendant now."

Hunter rubbed his chin. "I have just the guy for her."

"Mr. Valentine," the same young man who'd approached him earlier saddled up to their side. "We're going live in fifteen minutes."

"Thank you," Hunter said. He reached out and grabbed Camilla by her hand. She didn't try to, but their fingers linked naturally as he led her to the middle of the charging station.

"Here is where we will stand to cut the ribbon," he said.

"We?"

"Yes."

Camilla stuttered. "Um, I thought—I don't know if—"

Hunter chuckled. "Relax, gorgeous. You're a natural. Being on TV is your thing."

Camilla chuckled anxiously. "Yeah, but this is your business. I couldn't cut your ribbon."

"Why not?"

Camilla paused. "Well, you have a contract or something with Toyota. You're their hero. I'm sure they want you to carry out the celebration." Camilla's intake of breath almost made her dizzy. She looked for any excuse to be an onlooker like everyone else. Standing in front of Hunter now already threatened her nerves, never mind being at his side during a special occasion in his career.

"What's the real reason?" Hunter asked.

Camilla opened her mouth to speak but nothing came out.

"You don't want to be too close to me," he asked. "Do I smell?" Hunter lifted his arms and made a show of checking his scent.

"No, of course not. Don't be ridiculous," Camilla said, grabbing his arms to pull them down.

"Okay, listen." He grabbed her chin and drew her close. The move made her squirm and silently dismiss her sudden emotions. "I promise not to pester you, but I would love it if you would join me in cutting this ribbon today. Toyota won't mind. Our contract has nothing to do with this part of the occasion."

Camilla bit the corner of her lip as she thought it over. "I don't know, Hunter. It's a personal event."

Hunter stared at her for a moment. "You don't want to be personal with me, Angel? Because I'd like to become personal with you."

Camilla opened her mouth with a breathless gasp, and Hunter's eyes fell to her lips. A thrill of energy crawled around them both, and Camilla could do nothing but stare into his hypnotic eyes.

"If you keep looking at me like that, I'm going to kiss you, in front of all of these lovely people out here."

Camilla's cheeks flushed, and her heart rate increased,

but still she didn't pull her eyes away. She tried but it seemed useless when their connection was so strong.

Hunter took a step forward and leaned closer to her face. "I'm not kidding," he added, his voice deepening to a profound depth. Camilla seemed to snap out of her trance. She dropped her gaze and took a posterior step.

"Two minutes," someone shouted.

Camilla twirled toward her cameraman and called over Allison.

"Allison, this Hunter Valentine. Hunter, this is our assignment editor, Allison Sullivan."

"How are you, Allison?"

"I'm doing just fine, how about yourself, Mr. Valentine?"

Hunter took a sweeping gaze over Camilla. "Never been better," he said.

Allison smirked at Camilla then back to Hunter. "Thank you for inviting us. We appreciate the exclusive."

"Pleasure's all mine. Hey, Ms. Sullivan, you don't mind if I call you Allison, do you?"

"Not at all."

"Great, well could you do me a favor, Allison?"

"Sure, anything to help."

"Camilla is going to help me cut this ribbon, and we need you to catch it all on camera for us."

Allison smiled brightly over at Camilla, and her eyes lifted in surprise.

"I wouldn't mind at all," she said.

Camilla could almost roll her eyes. Allison was becoming more and more like Corinne every day. That wasn't a bad thing, but it was crazy at the same time.

"Merci," he responded.

"Sixty seconds," someone called.

Both Camilla and Allison slipped off to the side, but Hunter reached for Camilla.

"You'll stand over here with me, Angel."

"Right now? You don't want to do your introduction first?"

"With you by my side," he said.

Camilla glanced over at Allison and the other eyes that were trained on them.

"Okay…" she droned.

The camera counted down while a representative at Toyota did the same in hand signals. When they went live, Hunter's authoritative voice thanked the crowd and the viewers for being a part of the official partnership and grand opening between Toyota and VFC Energy. The audience cheered, and Camilla smiled proudly beside him. It was interesting really. They had only known each other a short spell but being in his company stirred things inside Camilla that she should've reserved for a boyfriend or fiancé.

That thought made her think about Steven, and Camilla fought to keep a frown off her face. As if sensing the brief cacophony in her spirit, Hunter turned to her with a smile just as Camilla heard her name. Her lips lifted at the corners, and the crowd cheered on as Hunter drew her in front of him and placed the giant scissors in her hand. He covered her hands with his massive palms, and a bustling heat crowded her fingers.

"Count down with me!" Hunter shouted to the crowd.

And they did loudly as Camilla and Hunter held giant smiles.

"3, 2, 1!"

The large blades sliced through the ribbon then fell to the ground as everyone around them cheered and flashes of light from camera crews ignited. A representative ran up and took the scissors out of their hands as Camilla eased to the side. Hunter slipped his arm around her shoulders and pulled her in for a celebratory hug. She reciprocated, slipping her arms around his solid waist.

"Thank you," he said in her ear, the heat from his mouth making her shiver.

"You're welcome. Thanks for allowing me to share that with you."

Hunter pulled back and gazed at her. With a slow grin, he replied, "Anytime, Angel. Anytime."

Chapter Fifteen

"*C*an I call you?"

Camilla stood on the sidewalk in front of WTZB's news van.

"I'd like that." She smiled, and Hunter returned her grin. "Congratulations. This partnership is a good thing for us all. You really are a great guy."

Hunter's gaze softened. "Thank you. You know I try to be, but that's according to who you question I guess."

"I can see it for myself."

Hunter reached for her chin and caressed the outline of her face, causing a ripple to sail down her flesh. She shuddered and took in a breath.

"Thank you for the roses," he said.

Camilla's smile widened, and a small giggle slipped from her lips. "Thank you for mine. I meant to tell you that at the club earlier this week, but I got a little sidetracked.

"What stole your focus?"

Camilla glanced away from him and cast her eye around the scenery. Although they landed on people in the distance, really, Camilla was inside her head, like she always was. She couldn't tell Hunter seeing him with Kelly had made her jealous, so she decided to take another route.

"If I ask you a question, would you be honest with me?"

"Of course."

Camilla's eyes drifted to his lips then back to his handsome face.

"The girl at the club, are you dating her?"

Hunter's brow creased a bit. "Kelly?"

"I guess. I don't know her name."

"No, she's just a friend."

"And by just a friend you mean you guys have a platonic relationship, or is she a friend with benefits?"

Camilla already knew the answer to this question. But Hunter didn't know she'd seen Kelly leaving his apartment the morning they met, so she held her breath to see if he would lie to her.

"Kelly and I aren't friends with benefits. We have been before, but she's not someone I'm dating nor currently seeing." Hunter held her attention. "Listen, Angel, I have no reason to proclaim false truths. I don't know what you've heard about me, and yes, I've been a bachelor for a long time, but I wouldn't lead you on. I told you that night at the club why you interest me and why I wanted to get to know you. You have every right not to believe me, but I wouldn't say that knowing I wasn't serious. Give me a chance before you give me a sentence."

Camilla's breathing held steady, and her eyes were trapped in his.

"Okay," was all she said.

Hunter smiled, a charming, primitive leer that was as contagious as he was. Camilla glanced away as she bit down on her bottom lip. The news van waited with Allison in the passenger seat and the cameraman behind the wheel.

"I'll call you, so pick up," he said.

Camilla nodded, and she turned and climbed into the van. Once buckled in, Hunter closed the sliding door and tapped the side twice. The van pulled away from the curb, and he watched it disappear down the street, thinking about how bad he'd wanted to kiss her. But she wasn't ready for that public display of affection. Not yet, Hunter determined. He'd wait until she trusted him and then there was no holding back.

Allison twisted in her seat to look at Camilla.

"If you don't turn around, your seat belt is going to choke you," Camilla said.

Allison laughed. "If I ever get too far into your business, and you don't want me there, just tell me to mind my business, but until then, I need the juice."

Camilla laughed and shook her head. "I swear you sound more and more like my best friend."

Allison nodded with a grand smile. "Hey, I can be your best friend, too. I'm all good."

They both laughed and so did the cameraman.

"You even have Alan laughing at you," Camilla said.

"Alan knows the deal by now," Allison responded. "So, this time, I won't question you to death, but I've got to tell you, honey, that man right there wants you bad. Honestly, I've been living in Chicago all my life, and I've never seen Hunter interact with a woman romantically. Have I seen him in pictures at an event with a woman on his arm? Of course, but in public like this, showing her off in front of the camera, whispering sweet nothings in her ear. Having her involved in a personal and professional venture of his?" Allison shook her head. "No, no, and no."

A blush fell over Camilla. "You could see all that?"

Allison nodded. "We all saw it, even the viewers at home."

Camilla didn't know how to feel about that. On the one hand, the more she spent time with Hunter, the more she wanted to stay, but she wasn't entirely sure that was a good thing. They rode back in silence with Allison sneaking a smirking peek back at Camilla every now and again. And Camilla could only think about the next time she would hear Hunter's voice again.

"SAY WHAT NOW?"

Corinne shifted the phone from one ear to the other. Camilla snickered.

"Hunter asked me out, but when I told him you were coming up for girls' weekend, he suggested we double date."

Corinne slipped a string of hair behind her ear. "With who?"

"I'm not sure. I told him we worked together before, but now you were a flight attendant—"

"A stewardess," Corinne corrected.

"Okay, a stewardess. What's your deal about being called a flight attendant?"

"Because it sounds so regular. I'll have you know I'm certified by the Federal Aviation Administration. I have a degree in social studies and communications and foreign language. I'm not just a flight attendant. I'm a stewardess."

"Honestly, Corinne, I don't think there is a difference."

"Yes, there is."

"I'm certain the definition is the same."

Corinne went to object again, but Camilla cut in.

"But, hey if stewardess is what you prefer, I promise to try and never regard you as a flight attendant again."

"Thank you."

"However, for the sake of getting through this conversation, you should know I told him you were a flight attendant. He seemed to have someone he thinks you'll get along with."

"He said that?"

"Not in those exact words but something close to it."

"Oh my God, it could be anyone but if it's one of his brothers..." Corinne purred. "I have never been the type to fawn over men, but those brothers are beyond beautiful, and educated. It's something about a sexy ass beautiful black man, and him being financially settled is like icing on the cake."

"I take it you'd be happy to go out on a date with one of his brothers then."

"Is that a joke?" Corinne asked, seriously interested in the answer.

"It's not!"

"Well it should be. If any of them are as intelligent as they're made out to be, do you know what that means?"

"I'm sure you're going to tell me."

Corinne laughed. "It means I could have an orgasm from a simple conversation."

Camilla balked and fell over laughing. She was sitting in the middle of her queen size platform bed dressed for bed. The two-piece top and bottom were made of black silk with a trim of lace crawling down the front of the top. It wasn't one of Camilla's sexier gowns, but it provided a simple, comfortable, and cute look. While she laughed at Corinne, Camilla couldn't help but think about why she wasn't wearing her cotton pajama top and bottom instead. Because over the last week, meeting Hunter made her want him in ways she shouldn't care to think about. If he knocked on her door right then, she would probably welcome him in, but somehow, she had to stop lusting after him long enough to really get to know him. Camilla was afraid of what might happen should that take too long. Besides that, Hunter still wasn't aware she lived in the only other apartment on the hall. To know he was so close played on Camilla's nerves.

She wiped the tears from her eyes. "Wow, there aren't many times that something shocks the hell out of me, but that was one of them."

Corinne chuckled. "I'm only telling the truth. You know the ratio of good men to toxic ones is just plain staggering." She paused. "Now, I have to Google his brothers."

Camilla laughed some more.

"What is so funny?"

Camilla wiped her eyes. "You are so serious about this. Corinne, you should really calm down. It's just a date."

"Let's make a deal."

"Oh no…" Camilla whined.

"Come on, let's make a deal."

"What about?"

"If by the end of our double date, you haven't had an orgasm, I'll never bring it up again."

Camilla shook her head as she laughed again. "You know, just to appease you, you're on." She chuckled. "I told the assignment editor at WTZB she reminded me of you."

Corinne perked up. "That means we'll get along great, I think."

Camilla chuckled.

"Is she coming on the date, too?"

"Oh no, although I think she has a crush on Lance."

"Look at you, know them by first name now. Have you met his brothers?"

"Not yet."

"Yet, huh?"

"I meant no."

"Girl, you don't have to backtrack on my account."

"Oh, look at the time, it's late, I should go."

Corinne laughed. "That's all right, I need my beauty rest anyway."

"Good night. I'll see you tomorrow afternoon!"

They both squealed. "It will be so good to have you here."

"Don't I know it."

They laughed again.

"All right, girl."

"Good night."

Camilla traced the edge of the phone and stretched out across her bed. Reaching down, she pulled the duvet cover up to her arms and rolled to the side. It was 11:42, and she wondered what Hunter was up to. *Go to sleep,*

Camilla. But sleep evaded her, and she drowned in a pool of risky thoughts.

Chapter Sixteen

THE NEXT NIGHT

"*I* need your address."

Camilla opened her mouth for a rebuttal, but Hunter continued.

"To take you out on a proper date, I need to come to your door and meet your parents."

Camilla laughed at his last statement.

"My parents don't live here."

With a smile on his face, he responded, "I thought it sounded good anyway."

Camilla tinkered out a giggle.

"Well, Mr. Valentine, Corinne and I are on our way down if you're ready. Meet us in the lobby."

Hunter didn't respond right away. Camilla didn't know it, but every time she rejected his quest to find out where she lived, it made her more attractive. Although he'd known from day one there was something different about Camilla, experiencing it first hand was gratifying. Those standards went to the moon and back with him, and if Camilla's objective was to make him uninterested, then she was doing a poor job of it.

Hunter swore he was going to figure her out. There was something magical about the atmosphere when they were together, and there was not a thing anyone could do to stop him from getting down to the bottom of it.

"We're waiting, sweetheart."

Camilla blushed. She turned around and glanced at Corinne. Her friend was robed in a black halter sleeveless sheath dress with clear pantyhose and three-inch Jimmy Choo's. Sterling silver jewelry accessorized her wrists, neck, and ears, and over her shoulders was a red faux fur mink. It covered her top then rode down to her thin waistline. Her hair sat in a Chinese bun on top of her head.

"We'll be there in a flash," Camilla responded.

"See you soon."

They disconnected the call.

"You look amazing," Camilla complimented.

"Thank you, sweetie. I'm merely a reflection of my best friend's glamour," she said.

Camilla smiled and twirled to look over herself one last time before they left. She'd pulled out the big guns tonight, cased in a long-sleeved silver glitter maxi dress with a plunging back that dipped down to the curve between her spine and ass. The glitter effect twinkled, and the lace pattern on her arms could be seen through to her brown skin. The knee-length dress feathered against her thighs with every movement she made, and instead of a mink, Camilla covered herself in a knee-length black belted trench coat. Her hair hung straight with razor sharp edges down to her shoulders, spilling over her back. A bang was trimmed just across her brows, making her look even more mystique. Light foundation was brushed across her face, and a coat of clear gloss covered her lips.

With every step she'd taken to transform herself, Camilla asked herself why. Why was she doing all of this anyway? That question was still lingering when the women grabbed their clutches and left the apartment. As they rode down, neither of them spoke. It was at the last moment when the elevator came to a stop that Corinne turned to Camilla.

"Remember our deal," she said.

The elevator doors opened on Camilla's smile, and she glided out of it with a search in her eyes. Just a few short inches away, she spotted Hunter taking a wicked examination over the entirety of her. His predacious assessment sent a blaze skating down her spine. He made appreciation have a whole new meaning. As if he could see through the fabric of the trench, Hunter analyzed, taking in her smooth bare legs and spike heels. She saw his jaw clench, and his scrutiny intensify then he approached her, and Camilla felt paralyzed.

His close-cropped haircut outlined his face, and his thick black brows only further accentuated his striking characteristics. Fine hairs interspersed around his mouth and jaw in the alteration of a mustache and expertly trimmed goatee. Hunter's attire matched the suave in his swagger. In a muted gray tailored jacket that cloaked his powerful arms and a white Tom Ford button down underneath, Hunter hovered right over Camilla, threatening her libido. Her eyes traveled down his masculine neck that was exposed from the two top buttons unclasped, to the light gray pocket square perched just inside his jacket pocket. A leather belt adorned his cut waist and muted gray pants rode his thighs to browse the top of his oxford shoes, capturing his cavalier-like receptivity with ease.

"You're the most gorgeous woman I've ever seen." His voice drummed across her skin.

Camilla laughed instantly. "Wow, what a compliment."

"Please take my word for it," he said.

She chuckled. "I do. And if I do say so myself, you're pretty gorgeous, too."

Hunter smiled mischievously. "Caution, if you continue to compliment me, I might get the wrong impression and think you like me."

Camilla pursed her lips and shrugged slightly. "Maybe I do."

Hunter winked. "Me too, beautiful." Hunter glanced at the man standing next to him. "This is my brother Xavier Valentine," he introduced. "Brother, this is Camilla Augustina. My angel."

It took too much work to keep the blush away. Camilla's cheeks filled with heat. "Good evening, Xavier," Camilla said. "It's nice to meet you. This is my friend, Corinne Thomas."

Xavier stepped forward; he'd barely glanced Camilla's way for drinking in Corinne's risqué look. "Good evening, ladies," he responded but kept his eyes on Corinne.

Standing across from him, Corinne smiled slow and

thoughtful. Her eyes also traveled over Xavier, and she could see the resemblance between him and Hunter. Mahogany brown skin, cascading in a milky way that disappeared behind a deep purple shirt with gold buttons that closed his formidable chest off to her. A black tailored jacket sat crisp over his broad shoulders with black pants, and classic black loafers settled on his feet. His ankles were revealed as the pants stopped right before the tongue of his shoe and a captivating gleam in his eye held Corinne firm.

"Good evening," Corinne replied. She glanced away briefly to acknowledge Hunter then returned her stare back to Xavier.

"Shall we?" Xavier held his arm out and stepped to her side where Corinne accepted, intertwining her limb with his.

They strolled side by side with Camilla and Hunter who had also slipped his hand down to the dip in her back and led them to a limo parked just beyond the revolving doors. Chicago's night air was slightly frigid with thin currents of strong wind. The ladies were escorted quickly to the door, and they both made haste getting inside. When they were sheltered in the heat of the back seat, they crossed their legs and glanced at their men.

Camilla's eyes scanned Hunter's strong chin and without trying, inhaled the spicy scent that drifted from him.

"You smell good enough to eat," she said.

Hunter turned his gaze to the flow of her throaty voice while at the same time Camilla couldn't believe she'd let those words spill out of her mouth. Since she'd been an adult, there weren't too many things that surprised her. But the provocative way she opened up around Hunter shook her every time.

His succulent lips spread into a devilish smile. "Let me know if you want a taste, and I'll be more than happy to oblige."

Heat flourished across her skin. It ironically bloomed from beneath her neck and spread equally over her flesh. A thumping between her thighs made Camilla writhe slightly, and the movement sent a pulsation beating over Hunter's skin. Camilla laughed a deep husky chuckle.

"You'll change your mind when you find out how greedy I am."

It was meant to turn the conversation back to safety, but it had the opposing effect. Camilla shut her lips tightly, realizing she was treading on dangerous grounds.

"I'm going to shut up now." She exhaled a long breath and looked away from him. The limo glided down the street to a destination unknown. She'd simply been told to dress semi-formal, so here she was putting her trust in a man she barely knew and following his lead. She'd already been to his house, on his job, really all she needed to do was get in his bed, and they'd be officially a couple.

That last thought made Camilla smirk.

"I rather enjoy hearing you voice your thoughts," Hunter said.

Camilla glanced back at his handsome face. "I don't know what it is about you, Hunter, but you bring out another side of me."

"Do you think that's a good or bad thing?"

Camilla kept a smirk on her face. "I'm not sure yet."

They stared at each other, and Hunter skimmed his fingers down the curve in her chin. His soft caress tickled Camilla's skin, and her eyes dropped then batted twice as their connection burned strong.

When the limo pulled to the entrance of The Violet Hour, Hunter removed his cell phone and powered it off. Camilla watched him with interest as he leaned forward and entered a code in a middle console. A small door slid out and he added his device inside.

"Are you leaving your phone in the limo?" she questioned.

Hunter glanced toward Camilla. "Yes, there are no phones allowed inside. Do you have yours?"

"Um, yes, I do."

"You don't mind leaving it, do you? I promise to keep it safe."

Camilla chuckled. It wasn't the phone she was worried about. It was the reason behind the rule that intrigued her.

"Not at all."

Reaching into her purse, Camilla retrieved her cell and powered it off. She handed it over to Hunter, and he added it in with his phone. Following their lead, Xavier and Corrine got rid of their phones, and the couples left the haven of the limo for The Violet Hour.

Chapter Seventeen

They were immediately seated upon entry. The ambiance of the club held mystery the deeper they journeyed inside. Curtains draped at the entrance of each salon they crossed into and candlelit tables sat throughout. Sleek, black, high back chairs were comfortably positioned, and chandeliers hung from the ceiling.

Camilla strolled across the hardwood floors coming to a stop at a table reserved for their party. It sat in front of a fireplace that was built into the wall across from them.

"Thank you," she said to the host as she went to take her seat.

"Would you like me to take your coat?" Hunter asked.

Camilla paused. "I'm going to leave it on for a second until I can shake off this chill," she said.

Hunter tilted his head in a nod then turned to the host.

"Thank you, Walter," he said.

"It's my pleasure, sir. Casey will be right with you."

The host gave a parting nod and left the table. Hunter took his seat next to Camilla no sooner than a blonde haired, blue-eyed woman glided up to their table.

"Good evening, how are you all tonight? I'm Casey. I'll be your server."

They all greeted Casey warmly, and she told them about their specials. Hunter leaned closer to Camilla and dipped his head.

"Do you mind if I order for you?"

She smiled back at him. "Not at all."

"Are you in for something light or with a little weight on it?"

Camilla's tongue traced the corners of her lips, and she pulled in a breath.

"I'll take something light. I wasn't sure if we were going to dine or not, so I ate a little bit before we left."

"Oh yeah, what did you have?"

"I make a mean jambalaya."

"No kidding?"

Camilla followed the outline of his mouth. "You should try it sometime."

"Is that an invitation?"

Before Camilla could respond, the server regarded him.

"And for you, sir?" Casey asked.

Hunter turned his attention to the waitress. "We'll have an order of stuffed dates and your Finocchio Focaccia."

"And to drink?"

"For my lady, The Riviera."

"And for you, sir?"

"I'll take The Dance of Dragons."

"Make that two," Xavier chimed in.

"Okay." The waitress finished entering their order. "Would your lady also like The Riviera?" the waitress asked Xavier.

"Yes," he spoke up then glanced at Corinne.

She nodded and winked, and the chemistry across the table was in full swing.

"I'll be right back with your orders."

"Thank you," they said in unison.

"The Dance of Dragons?" Camilla said.

Hunter eyed her. "It's rum, Amaro Di Angostura, and Falernum."

"Sounds strong."

A deep intoxicating chuckle trekked from him.

"I guess it depends on who's making it."

"That's true." Camilla glanced around. "Do you come here often?"

"It's my first time here."

"But you knew what was on the menu."

"I prepared beforehand."

"Hmmm. What made you chose this place and what do you suppose is the reason behind the no phones rule?"

"It's been one of those spots my brother, and I have wanted to try out. I can only guess the rule is, so their guests can enjoy a full experience in their ambiance without the disruption of a phone."

Camilla nodded then glanced at Xavier who was wrapped up in a conversation with Corinne.

"So, what do you think, Xavier?" Camilla asked.

Xavier brought his attention to Camilla. "I'll let you know by the end of the night," he said. Xavier's voice was just as strong as his brothers; however, it didn't give Camilla the same thrill.

Camilla took her attention back to Hunter. "And you?"

"As long as you're here, Angel, perfect."

Camilla blushed, and the waitress returned promptly with their drinks.

"So, what is it you do for a living, Xavier?"

It was Corinne who'd asked the question.

"I'm a sports agent amongst other things," Xavier said.

"Now that you mention it, I do remember seeing an article or two about you."

"Good things I hope."

"Maybe," Corinne teased, pulling a full-blown charming smile from Xavier.

Xavier glanced over at Hunter, and the men enjoyed a secret laugh.

"What's so funny?" Camilla asked.

Hunter cleared his throat. "My brother here was actually worried about being set up on a blind date." Hunter glanced back at Xavier and Corinne. "I think it's safe to say that is no longer the case."

"To my defense," Xavier said, "I've been set up on blind dates before, and none of them went over well."

"But, those were from your friends, not me."

"You're right." Xavier lifted his drink. "Cheers, brother."

Hunter lifted his in return. When the men took a drink, so did Camilla and Corinne. Both women eyed each other for a moment, and Corinne rose her brows as if to say, remember our deal.

"I didn't miss that," Hunter spoke up.

Camilla choked on her beverage, then cleared her throat.

"What didn't you miss?" she asked.

"That little silent communication you two had there. Is that something we should know about?"

The music in the venue changed, and Alicia Keys' "Fire We Make" sailed through the speakers.

"Ooh, that's my song," Camilla said trying to distract Hunter.

Like a charm it worked, or so she thought.

"Dance with me," he said, standing to his feet.

Camilla took another long pull of her drink then she accepted his proffered hand. While she untied the belt to her trench, Hunter studied her as she popped each button loose. When her garment was revealed, and Hunter received his first look at her dress, a shower of chills fled down his neck. Her perky breasts were halted just right against the thin material, and it shimmered over her curves like a piece of art in a museum.

"Let me," Hunter said, taking a few steps behind her to help remove the coat. It was then that he caught a look at the plunging back of her dress. His gaze smoldered as it followed the expressway of the sexy arch in her back. And it teased him, barely giving a peek of the hill that created her round ass. Hunter's mouth ran dry. With the women who showed their ass daily, whether in the news, on a beach vacation or on Instagram, none of them took his breath away like Camilla. She turned slowly around and met his hungry gaze. It was so rousing that Camilla's heart beat slammed against her chest as her nervousness was brought forth.

Hunter didn't say a thing. He couldn't. His thoughts were in a hail storm with every scenario in which this night could end. But the one he tussled most with was Camilla, in his arms, in his bed. He took a step forward, causing a stimulating brush of his chest to graze against Camilla's. Wrapping her in one solid arm, Hunter pressed her soft body against his. A thrill of chills scattered over Camilla. This energy of theirs was enough to knock her off her feet. Her hands rode up his torso and with a slow toss, Camilla's coat found its way against the seat of her chair. Her hair swayed against her shoulders as she looked up at him and wrapped her arms around his neck.

"You're the most beautiful girl in the world. Do you know that?"

Camilla smiled timidly. "I think you said that back at The Regency."

"Well I'm saying it again."

She giggled. "Thank you, handsome."

Hunter arched a sexy brow and wiggled them, making Camilla laugh. They moved to the dance floor, and the slow drag of the beat gave Hunter the opportunity to lift her hand and rotate her slowly as they moved.

Camilla didn't miss the virile way his eyes pierced her, and when he pulled Camilla in for a sway, she didn't miss the log in his pants that brushed against her crotch. She shuddered. Hunter's grazing palm slipped down her arms and outlined her waist. There they twisted their hips in a wine dance that sent an avalanche of heat coursing around them. Hunter felt like he'd struck gold. Everyone didn't get to live out their dreams. And the same went for finding a true soul mate. But this thing between them felt too natural to dismiss. He wanted to know everything about Camilla; her dreams and aspirations, her hopes and fears.

Hunter twirled her around then quickly pulled her completely against him again. "Tell me, Camilla, what is the one thing you've always wanted to do or see that you have yet to?"

A breathtaking smile covered her face, causing Hunter's heart to lug in his chest. "That's easy," she said. "But I don't know if now's the time to get into it."

Hunter regarded her longer. "Tell me," he prodded.

Camilla giggled. "So, demanding," she said jokingly.

"It's in my DNA, so it'll be something for you to get used to."

Camilla's brow rose. "You say that as if we'll be seeing more of each other."

"Won't we?"

Their conversation quieted as they both thought it over. Finally, Camilla smirked with a blush and dropped her face. When she looked back at him, soulful dark eyes watched back. She took in a breath and then spoke.

"I want to climb Mount Everest."

His thick brows rose, and Camilla couldn't hold in her laugh long enough to keep up the pretense.

"I'm just kidding. While I would like to climb a mountain, my first love would be to open a nonprofit business. A chain of hotels. They would be extended stay hotels and only open to the homeless."

Hunter's eyes widened. "I'm listening," he said intrigued by where this was going.

"So, in my head, I have this perfect plan," she continued as they danced in each other's arms. "Basically, everything would be documented as for who was staying, age, nationality, etcetera. The homeless who are able-bodied men or women would have to work off their stay by cleaning rooms and keeping the grounds of the establishment clean. Meals would be provided, breakfast, lunch, and dinner. And there would be a playground area for the kids." Camilla paused then moved on.

"I would also like to have a foundation to partner with that could help them get into the workforce and make a better life for themselves. The homeless that aren't able-bodied wouldn't have to clean, but if they can live without assistance then they would be responsible for allowing the clean-up crew to come in. This would be people in wheelchairs or that sort of thing."

Camilla's eyes bubbled as she spoke, and Hunter knew this was a passion of hers.

"The way I see it, there are hundreds even thousands, depending on which city you live in, of homeless people on the streets. The government doesn't want them there, the residents don't want them there, but no one is proactively helping. What better way to lend a helping hand in an area that desperately needs it? There are charities and non-profits for everything you can think of, but when it comes to the homeless, they're considered bottom of the barrel citizens, and though people say they care, their actions don't show it."

Camilla observed Hunter's amorous stare.

"That's not what you were expecting to hear, I guess."

He took his eyes to her lips. "No," he said. "Not at all. Maybe a luxury vacation in Sweden or Venice in the summer but never this."

"Those things would be nice, don't get me wrong, but when it comes to something I yearn to do, the nonprofit would be it. Sorry to disappoint you."

"You haven't disappointed me at all."

It was an infrequency for Hunter to lose his verbiage, but he was in such awe with Camilla that he could hardly keep up with the words he wanted to say.

"It's beautiful," he said. "You're beautiful, and I have a feeling I'll never meet anyone like you again."

Camilla blushed. "Thank you, but I'm not that different than you if you think about it. You're doing something environmentally for the human race and so am I," she paused, "possibly in the near future."

"You're right. We are alike in so many ways. Let me ask you, is this something you'd rather do on your own, or do you mind if I send you some contacts that might help you get started?"

Camilla's eyes widened. "Why would I mind?"

Hunter tilted his head slightly to the side. "Some women want to do things on their own, and fear if they have a helping hand it makes them unable to call their success accomplishments."

Camilla shook her head. "That's not me. Besides, this

nonprofit is not about me. Getting it off the ground is the best thing that could happen to our homeless community."

"You're truly inspirational right now, you know that?"

Camilla giggled. "And you're truly charming, Mr. Valentine."

The beat changed just as Hunter pulled Camilla in. He wrapped her in a snug embrace, and again, their hips moved together as they observed one another.

"Come home with me," he said.

Camilla's body heated more, and a pathway of festering nerves coursed down her vertebrae.

"Please," he begged.

His baritone voice scrubbed against her skin, making her nipples immediately recede. The harder they became, the more she shivered, and an intense pulsing coursed from her pussy.

"I… um…"

Hunter captured her lips, his tongue deep diving into her mouth. A rushing surge of scattered chills covered Camilla again, and when Hunter moaned a deep, thunderous growl, Camilla knew she was finished.

Hunter's hands sank into her back; his fingers riding the highway of her flesh down to her derriere. He was careful about his intentions, sinking a handful of her ass into his massive palm. The move was so meticulously snatching that one of his fingers nearly plunged into the crack of her ass, causing a delicious agony to rock against her core.

"Mmmm," she moaned as her hands explored his biceps, shoulders, and thick column that was his neck.

He almost lifted her right there, drawing Camilla so

close that she felt every sexual need there was to feel. A drip coaxed from her pussy, and when the music changed again, she pulled back, albeit slowly.

They panted, nearly out of breath as they took each other in. Camilla's brain was fried. Could she go home with him? Should she?

Taking a minor step back, she spoke, "I need to go to the ladies' room."

Before Hunter could reply, Camilla was gone. Running for the hills as if staying any longer would obscure her natural will.

Chapter Eighteen

*C*amilla pushed open the door of the bathroom and quickly shuffled to the sink. She took her hands through her hair and shook off a shiver. Looking at her reflection, questions flooded her brain. Did she really want to be one of those women who leave first thing in the morning after having a late-night rendezvous with a nameless guy in an emotionless romp? Camilla let out a breath.

Hunter was none of those things. Everything about him was moving, and within herself Camilla knew she wanted him. Sexually and everything else. *Oh my God, Camilla.* For a second, her thoughts shifted to Steven and the ass he'd made of her, but Camilla shook that memory, too. There wasn't anything wrong with having fun with Hunter. They were two consenting adults. To hell with Steven. She didn't owe him a thing, and this one time, she didn't feel like over-thinking it.

The door to the restroom opened, and Corinne sashayed inside. Camilla watched her friend strut to the stall of each bathroom door to check if there were any occupants inhabiting them. Once she'd finished her assessment, Corinne sauntered over to Camilla. Standing next to her friend, Corinne crossed her arms and leaned a shoulder into Camilla's shoulder.

"It happened, didn't it?" Corrine asked.

Camilla took her hands through her mane again.

"Go on, you can tell me."

Camilla smirked and bit down on her lip. "Hell yeah, it happened. On the dance floor."

"I told you," Corinne said in a sharp victory whisper.

"That's why you sought me out? To tell me you told me?"

"It's not the only reason."

Camilla took her eyes back to the mirror. "Well?"

"I came to make sure you were okay."

"Hmm."

"So, are you?"

"What does it look like?"

Corinne tinkered out a laugh. "Looks like Mr. Hunter Valentine may be getting lucky tonight. If that flushed look and those swollen nipples are any indication."

Camilla's eyes lurched, and she glanced down quickly at her breasts. Sure enough, they were puffed, and it didn't take an examination to know her nipples were stiff.

"What am I going to do, Corinne? This isn't funny."

Corinne frowned. "What else is there to do?"

Camilla gave her friend a frank expression.

"If you're asking me a serious question, I say go do the nasty." Corinne laughed, and Camilla's cheeks filled with heat. Seeing her friend distressed, Corinne became serious. "Okay, look, ask yourself a few questions. I know you don't want to appear easy or like any of the greedy bimbos I'm sure he's had. So, do you like him?"

"I wouldn't be on this date if I didn't."

"Okay, do you think he's only after you for some ass?"

Camilla opened her mouth, but with incomplete thoughts, she paused. "I don't know. How am I supposed to know that?"

"Okay, scratch that question, but answer this. Would you care if he did?"

Camilla took a spell to respond.

"Be real with me here."

"Maybe, just a little."

Corinne sighed. "What do you want, Camilla?"

Camilla looked back at her reflection, but there was no question about what she wanted. With acquiescence, Camilla fixed a few strands of hair that were out of place and washed her hands. After drying them, she glanced at Corinne.

"Let's go," she said, reining in her resolve.

The two ladies exited the restroom and strolled back to their seats where Hunter and Xavier stood enveloped in a conversation.

"I hope we didn't keep you fellas waiting too long," Camilla said.

With a smile, Corinne added. "Yeah, that would be a shame."

The men eyed the women.

"Actually, I was just telling Xavier how much of a bore he was," Hunter said.

They laughed, and Corinne responded, "I don't' believe that."

"Your food's cold," Hunter said to Camilla.

"Well, I'm not hungry for food," she implied in a deep flirtatious voice.

Hunter's lids dropped, and his eyes darkened like molasses. For a split second, he acknowledged Xavier.

"You two will be all right getting home, won't you?"

Camilla felt a thrill crawl down her back.

"For sure," Xavier responded, "as long as Corinne doesn't mind keeping me company longer."

"I don't," Corinne responded.

"In that case…" Hunter reached for Camilla's trench then closed in on Camilla and brushed the tips of his fingers across her chin. "Angel," he said.

Camilla blushed and twirled around allowing Hunter to help her inside her jacket.

"Till we meet again," Hunter said to Corinne and Xavier.

They took their leave, and Camilla reminded herself to breathe. This was what she wanted. Everything would be okay.

SHE HAD UNDERESTIMATED the nerves in her psyche. Sitting next to Hunter put Camilla so on edge that every now and again she'd shift in her seat. The last person she was with sexually was her fiancé, and it felt like decades since she'd been with anyone else. *Jesus, get a grip, Camilla.* She tried, but it didn't work out so well. Camilla stared out the window, giving Hunter almost no contact.

"Are you okay?" his thick voice grooved.

She turned her attention to him and swallowed quickly then nodded a response.

"Are you sure?" Hunter glanced down at the space between the two and the way Camilla had almost drawn up.

She exhaled. "I… I don't know," she finally admitted.

"Is there anything I can do to make you feel better?"

His voice was easy and relaxing. Camilla sank against her seat.

"Honestly, it's not you that's making me feel crazy." She paused and thought it over. "Well, it is you, but not directly, indirectly if you know what I mean." Camilla sighed. She was rambling, and sure Hunter didn't know what she was talking about.

He reached for a champagne glass and filled it to the rim, then handed it over to Camilla. She accepted it, taking it down faster than she'd ever swallowed anything. Hunter arched a brow and refilled her glass.

"Thank you." She sipped on that one and watched as Hunter filled a glass of his own.

"Come here," he said.

Camilla scooted over until their thighs brushed, and Hunter draped his arm across the top of the seat. Camilla took down the rest of her champagne then looked up at Hunter.

"You don't mind if I have more, do you?"

He regarded her. "If you want more, I'll give you more."

He refilled her glass and watched her take it halfway just as the limo pulled to The Regency entrance and parked. Hunter glimpsed down at her hand and saw it tremble.

"Camilla."

She looked over at him.

"You don't need to get drunk to spend a night with me. If you've changed your mind, I won't be offended. You're allowed to change your mind."

Camilla stared at him then dropped her head.

"Hunter, I'm so sorry."

He lifted her chin. "Let me walk you to your door."

She nodded, and they exited the limo and strolled inside. Standing at the bank of elevators, Hunter folded his hands behind his back as they stood side by side. The doors opened, and Hunter waited for her to enter.

She glanced over at him. "I'll catch the next one."

Hunter stared at her face. "I'm not leaving you in the lobby while I ride up. So, you can get on without me, or we can go up together."

Camilla nodded then stepped into the elevator. Hunter moved in behind her, and they rode to the fifth floor where Camilla exited.

"Hunter, again, I'm sorry to be so indecisive," she said before stepping off. "It's just, I haven't been with anyone since my..." she paused, and Hunter held her attention. "I've been with a single person for the last decade or two, so it's not easy for me."

Hunter nodded once. "I understand, and I would like to see you again if that's possible."

Camilla didn't know why she was surprised. All Hunter had shown was that he was a pretty standup guy, but all the same, it did amaze her. Most men would probably run and never look back if they were in the same situation. Camilla's forehead creased, and the doors to the elevator threatened to move if she didn't hurry and exit.

"You want to see me again," she asked for clarification.

"Yes."

Camilla hesitated. "Okay... I'll call you."

Hunter smiled. "I'll look forward to it, Angel."

She stepped outside the elevator and watched him as the doors closed. The numbers over the top ticked as he ascended to their floor, and Camilla wondered if she'd just made a mistake.

Chapter Nineteen

$\mathcal{S}$he paced the stretch of the hallway, musing over stormy thoughts. *What are you doing?* She didn't know. Her mind traveled to Corinne, and the words she'd spoken shortly before they left the restroom.

"What do you want, Camilla?"

Camilla stopped pacing and sulked. She wanted to be with Hunter, but not just physically. If that's all he wanted, Camilla would be more hurt than she was willing to admit. *But he asked to see you again.* But it could be all for the chase. *You have one life to live. What's the worst that could happen?* Camilla shut her eyes and fought with ironclad strength to clear her musings.

After another long moment, she went back to the elevator and rode up to the top floor. When the doors opened, Camilla stuck her head out then exited quietly. Her footfalls were soft as she padded down the hallway, stopping just in front of her door, but she didn't move to go inside. Instead, her feet turned, and she strolled a little ways to stand in front of Hunter's door. Camilla's heart rocked as she faced the wooden barrier and blew out a staggering breath. If she knocked on his door, Camilla better be damn sure of it this time.

Without giving herself time to consider it, Camilla turned and walked away. Her hand dove into her clutch, desperately looking for the keys as her speed increased and she made a fast escape. It was the soft unlocking click of his door combined with a current of wind that moved past her down the hallway that let Camilla know he was there.

"Don't leave."

The depth in Hunter's voice caused a crusade of heated chills to fall down her form. She stood right next to her door but not facing it, so in hindsight she just appeared to be merely running away but not fast enough. The floorboard of the carpeted corridor didn't make a sound, but still Camilla could feel him getting closer. The heat from his aura was like a compelling wave that connected them whenever they were near. When one of his thick hands slid up Camilla's arm to her shoulder, followed by the other, Camilla's eyes closed, and she carefully pulled in an elongated breath before releasing it in much the same manner.

Gently, Hunter drew her into the sanctuary of his broad chest, and when her shoulders brushed across his skin, she trembled.

"I can't," she said, fighting like all hell with wanting to be with him but refusing to become another score on his belt.

"But you want to," he replied. "Or you wouldn't be here."

Camilla's chest rose and fell slowly. "Doesn't mean I should which is why I'm leaving. I've had too much to drink. I need to think with a clear head. I don't do this."

Hunter's lips met the top of her ear. "Are you frightened of me, Camilla?"

"Should I be?"

"Answering a question with a question. I thought we were past that."

"We? You make us sound like a couple."

"How can we be if you don't take a chance and open up to me."

"I'm trying."

"Are you sure about that?"

Camilla didn't respond, only searched for the right words to say.

"Camilla," he squeezed her tighter, "I want to know you. Is that going to be a problem for you?"

"No," she said without hesitation.

"You can trust me."

Camilla shook her head with a smirk. "It's not that I don't trust you, it's late. What other reasons would I come to your place besides... besides..."

"Why did you come?"

Camilla blinked rapidly. "I'm not sure."

"But you are."

An upsurge of heat flowed between the two, melting them together.

"Hunter..."

"I'll take care of you."

She turned around to face him and was caught up in the dark treacle of his searing gaze. *Damn it.* She was toast. Her plight would've been better assessed if she hadn't face him. Hunter's hand slipped down her arms then his fingers slinked into hers, and together they moved into the privacy of his suite.

"WOULD you happen to have more champagne?"

They were sitting in Hunter's den on a black sofa in front of a fireplace. Hunter strolled to the bar and retrieved a champagne flute and a short glass. He lifted a bottle of Ace of Spades and popped the cork. Champagne fizzed to the spout, and quickly, he poured her a glass.

"So, you've always wanted to climb Mount Everest," he asked, turning to tread across the room to her.

"I told you I was kidding."

"But I knew you weren't."

A small smile covered Camilla's face, and she accepted the glass he offered. "I've had the silly thought of climbing mountains ever since a trip I took with my father when I was ten. We were in the Alps, and I'd watched a group begin their ascent. I thought it was fascinating. It was the perfect weather, semi out in the open, with nature calling." She took a sip of her champagne as Hunter took a seat with his own dark concoction in hand. "I vowed to do that someday."

Hunter loved the glow on her face. "You just become sexier by the minute."

Camilla laughed melodically, and it played on his chest like piano keys.

"You're turned on about seeing me climb a mountain?"

"Yes, ma'am, but you aren't climbing a mountain without me."

Camilla's smile turned coy, and she leaned slightly his way and took a hand down his solid thigh. A giggle escaped her as a buzz crawled from her fingers down her arm. "Why is that," she asked huskier than she realized.

At the moment, Camilla couldn't care to notice because whether it be the many glasses of champagne finally catching up to her or the intense carnal awareness in the room, her initial reason for coming to Hunter's place resurfaced.

"Because you need security."

"Oh, do I?"

"Yeah."

Camilla giggled again and drank the rest of her champagne. "So," Camilla stood to her feet and started a slow stroll across the room, "are you up for giving me a tour of your place?"

Hunter stood, and with glass in hand cruised to her side.

"I'd love to. You've seen the kitchen and dining area. "You've also seen the living room."

"But not the complete hall."

"You're really intrigued by that mural, aren't you?"

"Isn't that the reason you had it drawn, to be intriguing?"

"Not in essence," he said. "This way."

With a hand to the small of her back, Hunter led

Camilla through the living room, down the corridor where the flowers on the wall bloomed and a name in the sky read Trevor. Neither of them spoke as they passed, but Camilla did get a glimpse of the skyline through the window.

"Beautiful," she mentioned.

"I did ask the owner if there was another apartment with my view."

"Did you?"

"I did."

"No such luck?"

Hunter smiled down at her. "Unfortunately, no."

"Aww, it was worth a try."

They trailed into a back room.

"Going after anything your heart desires is worth a try," he said.

Camilla stopped walking to look at him. "Anything?" she asked.

"Anything." He took his gaze from her face and hit a switch on the wall. "This is my theater room."

Camilla didn't wait for a second to scan the room as she took a few steps up to him, stood under his shadow, and leaned into his chin.

"Kiss me, Hunter."

Hunter studied her for a second. "Are you sure about that, Angel?" His thick voice ticked. "Be careful about your response. I won't ask a second time."

Camilla responded by pressing her breast against his torso, and concurrently, Hunter's hands grazed up her neck, drawing Camilla in with such force she practically yelped.

His mouth plunged into hers, sucking her in like they

were meant to breathe as one organism. It was as if he'd been holding that ravenous attack back, and it burst the minute she gave him permission. He savored Camilla and swallowed her whole as her body flamed against his. Hunter's hands trotted over her shoulders, down her back, and he lifted Camilla with a handful of ass. Her legs instinctively wrapped around his cut waist.

"Mmmm, ah!" Camilla chimed, sucking in a lungful of air when their mouths parted.

Hunter rained kisses down her neck and bit into her flesh. He turned and left the theater room and headed down another corridor. At the entrance, he moved through the dark space that was only bathed in a stream of glowing moonlight. At the bed, Hunter laid her down, and Camilla watched him remove his shirt. She bit her lips as his fingers traveled down its seams, and he peeled it off his shoulders.

The magnificence that was his chest transcended into a cord of stacked muscle that Camilla would only assume Zeus could maintain. It fit him so immaculately, anything else would've been unsuitable. When Camilla's eyes traveled to his toned waist, she had to wonder what was hiding behind those pants, and it didn't take long for her to find out.

Hunter disrobed fully, as if she were an audience, and he was performing a striptease. His thighs were just as powerful as she knew they would be, and his dick sprang forth with a curve at the tip. A wave of heat crawled down Camilla's skin, and she sat forward and trailed her fingers down his abs. She kept it moving, sinking to his pelvis to grab a handful of dick. An animalistic sound crept from

Hunter's throat, and he took a step back as Camilla sank to her knees.

She covered the circumference of his head with her mouth and sucked in tightly with her tongue. Another growl trekked from him, and Camilla opened her throat and devoured more of his member.

"Mmmm," she moaned. His skin was so soft and smooth, but detrimentally rigid on her palette. With her hand, she stroked the bottom half of his shaft as her head bobbed and weaved to meet up with her closed fist.

"Shi-it!" Hunter's head fell back, and his hand gripped her hair and coached her rhythm as he fucked her mouth.

"Mmmm." Camilla salivated as she took in a considerable amount of his engorged erection. The act was so erotically charging that her pussy pulsed, and her nipples became sore as they hardened.

"Fuck me!" Hunter shouted, pulling Camilla off his cock and yanking her into his arms.

Her legs wrapped around his waist, and she held on to his neck. "Yes," she said breathlessly, "Fuck me."

Their mouths crashed into one another, fiercely, like savage animals unable to get enough. Hunter was completely naked where Camilla was still in her dress. He sought to find her a way out of it, but the task took longer than either of them had the patience of waiting.

"Rip it, I don't care, get it off," Camilla panted.

Hunter walked them to a wall and pressed her against its base. Hungry, needy hands gripped the material from the front, and it shredded slowly with each thread pulling apart with a splitting grind. Camilla didn't know it was possible to be more turned on than she was right now, but after the fabric fell from his fingers, her arms wrapped around his neck, and she had a desperate need to be filled with him. Their lips sank together, and the heat from their mouths spread across their faces as Hunter bent his hips and dug into her sweet heat. Camilla's mouth opened on an intake of breath and without giving her a chance to exhale, Hunter sank farther into her womb, sliding into a seal of wet warmth.

An outcry poured into his mouth as Camilla shouted from the intense intrusion. He shuddered then peered at her as his lips stopped moving against hers. Their eyes locked and held as Hunter rotated his hips and dug deeper, connecting with her G-spot.

"Oh my God," she whispered against his mouth, and Hunter moved out then in again, finding a tempo with resplendent ease. "Ooh…" Camilla moaned, and her eyes rolled.

Hunter's pace increased, and the curve in his head speared and mixed with her nectar. Camilla's toes curled, and she purred at his sweet beating. Back and forth, in and out, his expanded shaft punched into her, stroking her walls within. Hunter watched the beautiful way her face glowed in ecstasy as he drove into her canal. It intensified his resolve, and he took her harder than intended against the wall. Her back leaned against the base as she kept her hips elevated, taking every inch of his masterful plunges. The sound of their joining clapped in reverberation around the room as Hunter found a home inside her inner recesses.

He dug and dipped, making sure not to leave an inch of

her womb undiscovered. Camilla's head rolled, and she lost her breath with each jagged thrust she endured. Hunter fucked her and nibbled along her chin as he stood on the tips of his toes to explore the furthest reaches of her cove.

"Aaah! Oh my God..." she panted.

"Tell me what your heart desires, and you shall have it," he said, continuing to grind her with the madness of a starving patient.

Camilla's response was a dragging moan as Hunter lifted her higher, fucking her at extreme angles.

"Ah! Shit!" she screamed. "Hunter! Oh my God..."

"Tell me," he reiterated.

"Nothing, nothing," she mumbled. "You, that's it."

Her head fell back as Hunter's thrusts pummeled into her core, beating against her so innately that a sharp tingle fled in a freeway from her clitoris up her spine and back.

"Oh God, I'm going to come!" She screamed, and Hunter stroked her faster, giving Camilla the most blissful orgasm, she'd ever had in her life.

"Aaaah, Hunter!"

Her body jerked from the force of her release, her cream covering him instantly, causing Hunter to come also.

"Sh-it!" he barked. Hunter recaptured her mouth, and they moaned and bounced against each other as their vibrations exploded.

A constellation of stars took over Camilla's sight as she breathed with him, totally encapsulated by his undertaking. Holding her firmly against him, Hunter removed her from the wall and strolled over to the bed for round two.

Chapter Twenty

$\mathcal{I}$t was the smell of early morning bagels that woke Camilla. She stretched with the prowess of a cat, and her limbs were so relaxed it was as if she'd had a full body massage. Camilla blinked open her eyes, and they scurried over the black and gold sheets. Rising to a sit, Camilla tossed a layer of hair away from her face and took her eyes across the contemporary room.

Hunter's furnishings were very manly with dark patterns that sat throughout. Camilla could liven it up a bit in here. Give it a woman's touch so to speak, but just as she had the thought, she realized how silly it was. Camilla would need to be his woman to do that. She tossed her legs over the bed and tiptoed into his bathroom. Inside, she searched for an extra toothbrush then smiled when she found one laying out undoubtedly for her. She pushed her hand against the door then leaned over the sink; the ache between her thighs made last night's memories flourish through her mind.

Camilla took in a deep breath then turned on the faucet and prepared her toothbrush for use. She brushed and watched herself in the mirror then took off the large shirt she'd put on sometime between their sexcapades through the night, opting not to wait till she got home for a bath. She traipsed to the shower and turned it on, then slipped inside. She held her face under the downpour of water, letting the heated drops knead into her skin. Camilla was there no longer than sixty seconds when she felt movement behind her.

"Am I interrupting?" Hunter said from the shower door.

Camilla turned to face him then reached to pull him in. He came willingly, completely disrobed and unabated. Seeing every inch of him in the light of day came with a delectable sight. His body was just as tone, rigid, and perfectly carved the way it felt last night. However, covering the details of his makeup mangled her and hijacked her heart beat.

"Did I tell you last night how beautiful you were," he asked.

"I'm sure but my memory hasn't caught up with me yet."

"What do you remember?"

Camilla dipped her lids. "I remember you and me, in there," she said.

"Hmmm. And what else?"

"I remember giving you a hard time, too. Sorry about that."

"Don't be sorry." His hands reached for her neck. "It was my pleasure to give you a hard time back." He drew her to him, and his lips landed on her as they stood right underneath the water.

His hand traveled down her side, and he gripped her thigh and lifted her leg. With his other hand, he released her neck, and it followed the same path to her other thigh. When he hauled her, she strung her arms over his shoulders and leaned into his chest. Their lips locked in a passionate, heated kiss. They liquefied as Hunter submerged inside Camilla's heated harbor. The ache that derived from last night strengthened into a delicious penetrating throbbing.

Hunter held on to her ass, plunging with ease as he lifted then drove into her wet cocoon, sending a revolution of tingles spiraling down her backbone with each magnanimous thrust.

"Oh my, my, my, my God!" she stuttered as water dripped into her mouth.

"You are so fucking beautiful," Hunter said, sucking in a mouthful of her areolas.

"Hunter..." she purred. "Oh my God, baby." Her words were fluent but soft and caught in a rapture that left her floating in a cloud.

His grind was extreme, impassioned, and driven, so much so that they exploded before they had time to slow their pace and settle into a pattern.

"Be with me," Hunter said, nibbling on her bottom lip.

Camilla gazed at him with her lids low. "I am with you," she said.

"That's not what I meant." He kissed her softly. "Be with me, Angel. I want you to be my girl."

Camilla's heavy gaze stilled then rose by an inch.

"Be, your girlfriend?"

Hunter kissed the side of her face, the edge of her jaw, and the back of her neck. "Yes," he confirmed. "Don't think about it, just tell me yes."

"Yes," she heard herself say.

Hunter paused his kisses and pulled his gaze to hers.

"Do you mean it?"

"Do you?"

"I wouldn't play around with—"

"I know. I think," she paused. "I know," she confirmed. "I wouldn't say yes if I thought you would."

The corners of his lips lifted, and a pleasurable glimmer shone in his eye.

"I knew you wanted me all along, girl."

Camilla gasped, and Hunter guffawed. She pursed her lips and rolled her eyes then couldn't help but join in on his contagious laughter. They exited the shower after washing each other than robed lightly and had breakfast. The conversation covered sports, politics, and even religion. With opposing views on some things, neither Hunter nor Camilla were caught up in a tit for tat.

When the day turned into night again, Camilla took out her cell phone and checked her history. Six missed calls from Corinne who was currently inside her apartment.

"I am a terrible friend," Camilla said as she sat underneath Hunter while they watch *The Best Man* on TV One.

"No, you're not," he replied.

"How can you say that when I've left Corinne at my apartment all day. She came up from Florida to spend the weekend with me, remember?"

Hunter looked over at Camilla. "Damn, you are a bad friend."

She gasped again and swatted him as he laughed and ducked to get out of her path. "I'm just kidding, woman, don't maul me." He turned quickly to cover her hands and arms.

Camilla poked her lip out, and Hunter sucked it into his mouth. "You know this will happen every time you stick your lips out at me."

"Mmm, I don't think I mind."

They kissed slowly and softly. This had been one of the best days Camilla endured in a long time, and it was real. Hunter had asked, and she'd agreed to be his girlfriend. She was in a real relationship. Her heartbeat spun as she took it all in and reveled in the heat of his mouth.

"I KNOW you are not even trying to sneak in this house for real."

Corinne sat on the white leather sofa with her arms folded across her chest. On the television, *Love and Hip Hop* streamed across the screen.

"I'm not sneaking in," Camilla countered.

"So, what do you call turning the click in the keyhole silently then tiptoeing inside?"

"I just didn't want to disturb you should you be getting some shut-eye."

Corinne turned around in her seat and eyed the time. "At noon on a Sunday? Try again."

"Well I don't know what you and Xavier got into, so I was just being cautious."

"Mmhmm, yeah. You would've known what happened between Xavier and I had you decided to come home yesterday. You know, anytime during the full 24 hours allotted to us by the Most High."

Camilla stuck her lips out. "You've made your point." She strolled down the hallway with Corinne quickly following behind her.

"So, what's the word?" Corinne asked.

Camilla dropped her heels at her bedroom entrance and turned to face her friend. Folding her arms across her chest, Camilla's serious expression developed into a full-blown grin.

"He asked me to be his girlfriend."

Corinne's eyes popped, and she reached out and shoved Camilla. "Shut up!"

Camilla glanced down at her shoulder with a frown then back to Corinne. "Assault much?"

Corinne squealed and shoved her again, and Camilla couldn't help but laugh.

"You get on my nerves," Camilla said, pivoting and skipping to her bed. She fell down in the middle of the mattress with her arms stretched wide.

"It was so unexpected," Camilla said dreamily. "I don't even know why I'm this excited."

"I do."

Corinne crawled on to the bed and folded her legs beneath her. Camilla glanced up at her.

"Why?"

"Because you're being proved wrong. The image you have of him in your head; you know that playboy, unattainable bad idea image. Yeah, as the days past, he proved that he just might be a caring, understanding, one-woman man who most women hope an alpha male like him could be. And his eyes are on you."

Camilla pondered Corinne's words. She was right, but there was something else. With that excitement was real fear. How long would Hunter's eye be on her? Was she the only one, or would she be naïve to believe he wouldn't date anyone else while they were together.

"I said yes so quickly. What if it is a bad idea?"

"Then you'll learn from it. It's too late now, you're in it to win it."

"Gee thanks." Camilla continued to ponder. "He wants me to meet his mother." Camilla glanced over at Corinne just in time to see her eyes lurch again.

Corinne placed a hand on her chest, shook into silence.

"Don't stop giving me your almighty advice now."

"This is more serious than I thought," Corinne said.

"I'm nervous as hell, and I can't seem to tell him no. It's becoming an addiction. Maybe Hunter is bad for my health."

A jiggling laugh began in Corinne's belly and chuckled up her throat.

"Damn, girl, you are scared, huh."

Camilla squeezed her eyes closed tight.

"Come on, Corinne. I've known him all of what a week and a half. We just decided to be a couple and that was a decision made in the throes of…"

Corinne leaned back with an arch in her brow. "Oh no, don't stop on my behalf. In the throes of what?"

With her eyes closed, images of Hunter's tenacious undertaking sailed to the forefront. The tight clasp his manly hands had on her as his fingers dug into her skin. The rocking of his hips as he thrust calamitous strokes into her core. The saccharine way his tongue tasted; heated, wet, and euphoric. Camilla bit down on her lip and squirmed.

"Dayum!" Corinne shouted.

Camilla opened her eyes sharply. "What happened," she said, rising to her elbows to look around the room.

"You do know you were just rocking your hips and biting down on your lip, right?"

"Oh my God," Camilla said, exasperated as she fell back into the mattress.

"Ooou, girl, I aspire to feel the level of ecstasy that you feel right now."

"He said she'll love me."

Corinne blinked. "Who, his mom?"

"Yeah. He said, and I quote, "She will love you.""

Camilla turned her head up to look at Corinne again.

"Look, here's my advice even though you didn't ask for it," Corinne began. "If it makes you feel uncomfortable to meet his parents, then tell him. It's too early in your relationship, and you think you both should what until you've dated for a while."

Camilla repeated Corinne's statement. "It's too early in our relationship, and we should both wait until we've dated for a while."

"Yeah, see, you've got it."

Camilla's phone rang, and she'd rose from the bed and skipped over to it. Upon seeing Steven's number, Camilla frowned. "You would think he'd give up by now."

"That must be Steven."

Camilla tossed her phone and trod back to her bed. With them both deciding to ignore Steven, they changed the subject.

"Okay, since we missed a whole day together, let's go out for happy hour." Corinne glanced at her watch. "I still have a few hours before my flight, and I can tell you all about my time with Xavier."

Camilla smiled and nodded. "Let me get ready."

"Fast, times a ticking!" Corinne said at Camilla's retreating back.

Chapter Twenty-One

"It's too early in our relationship, and we should both wait until we've dated for a while."

Camilla exited WTZB, repeating the statement Corinne had come up with the day before. Hunter was picking her up from work today, they would have dinner then head home, but during their meal Camilla planned to tell him that meeting his parents would have to come at a later date. She had a mind to ask if all the women he dated met his parents. If so she could breathe easy that meeting them wasn't a big deal. But somehow, Camilla knew that not to be true, and the last thing she wanted was to insult him.

She was wrapped in her musing so tightly that she padded down the steps without watching her surroundings. It was when a tall figure cut her path short by standing in front of her that Camilla froze, and the blood in her face drained like she'd seen a ghost.

"So, you plan to just keep ignoring my calls?"

Her shock turned into anger so quick Camilla didn't recognize herself.

"What the hell, Steven!"

Steven lingered over her in a double-breasted beige coat with shades strewn across his eyes.

"What are you doing here!?" Camilla glanced around then grabbed Steven's hand and pulled him to the side of the building.

"I wouldn't have popped up on you like this if you had taken one of my calls."

Frustrated, Camilla massaged her temples.

"How could you just up and leave everything we had behind and move to Chicago? I had to find out from a clip on CNN that you're working for this news station."

"Steven, I don't give a damn how you found out. There is nothing to hold on to back in Florida. No me, and no you. I can't believe you just showed up like this."

"What is a desperate man to do when his wife won't answer the phone."

Camilla waved her hand in the air. "Oh, Steven, just stop it!"

Steven let out a frustrated breath. "Baby, you know me. Every now and then, I need to be put in check, but you know I'm not going anywhere." He stepped closer to her. "I love you."

Camilla thought she was going to be sick. Steven thought love was breaking off their engagement whenever he supposedly needed to be put in check, and even worse, he actually expected Camilla to deal with it.

Camilla reined in her sanity and spoke with a clear concise voice, "Look, I really don't want to argue with you about this, especially not here."

Camilla glanced back at WTZB to see if anyone lingered at the entrance, but no one did.

"Then let's go back home. I have a flight with both of our names on it." Steven glanced down at his watch. "If we leave now, we can make it. If not, we'll have to take anoth—"

"Stop it! Just!" Camilla let out a deep breath. She couldn't deal with him. Steven would just keep acting like everything was okay. "You don't get it," she said, feeling defeated.

Steven stepped even closer to her; so close she could smell his Old Spice cologne. He grabbed her by the waist and leaned closer to her face. But Steven wasn't expecting her rejection, and when she pushed off his chest, his calm nature turned cold.

"Get your ass over here," he said, reaching again to grab hold of her.

In a blur, Camilla scurried around Steven, but was yanked back when he grabbed her arm.

"Get off me, Steven!" Camilla jerked her arm free and stared at him in disbelief. "What the hell is wrong with you!?"

"You are what's wrong with me, and if I have to tell you again—" Steven's words were cut short, and he glared at something over Camilla's shoulder. "What the hell are you looking at?"

Camilla rotated on her heels and was confronted by a

menacing, brooding Hunter Valentine that sent daggers with his gaze over at Steven. Camilla opened her mouth for an explanation of why Steven was there, and what was going on, but the death stare Hunter fixed on Steven was so ominous it made Camilla think of retreating. When his eyes traveled to hers, instantly his gaze thawed, and the warmth that she'd always recognized returned.

"Are you okay," he asked.

Camilla swallowed thickly since her tongue felt like sandpaper.

"Yes." She paused. "I can explain." Her voice was just beyond a whisper, but at the moment, Hunter wasn't interested in her explanation. He lifted her arm and looked it over, then with effortless ease, removed her from his front to hide her behind his back.

His gaze darkened again, and Camilla tugged at his bicep. "Please, Hunter, don't."

"Who do you think you are?" Steven asked.

"Steven, is it?" Hunter said. "The only reason you walk away today with your face intact is because my Camilla works here. So, consider yourself lucky. The stars are aligned in your favor. But understand something. If you ever put your hands on her again, I'll rip your motherfucking shoulder off. Am I clear?"

Steven was partly pissed, but mostly anxious trying to figure out if Hunter was serious. He made a bad decision to test out the theory.

"Your Camilla?" Steven stepped to Hunter. "That's where you're mistaken, my man. Camilla is my wife, she belongs to me!" Steven attempted to reach around Hunter in an effort to get hands on Camilla. Hunter sent one fast blow to Steven's chest, and Steven flew back a foot and tilted on his heels as he fought to recover the oxygen that had just been bullied from his body.

"Oh my God!" Camilla shouted.

Hunter stepped to Steven again, but smartly, Steven recoiled while still taking a massive effort to refill his lungs with air.

"Please, Hunter, let's go!"

Camilla tugged at his arm again, and Hunter thought better of killing the man in the parking lot. He turned toward Camilla, and without another word started toward his Maserati Quattro Porte. With Camilla at his side, the two hustled to get into his vehicle, and when Hunter slipped into the driver's seat the madness he felt radiated from him.

Hunter checked his rearview mirror then sent a glare back across the parking lot. He didn't say a word, and in the next instance, they were riding down the boulevard. Camilla shut her eyes. What a disaster that had been. But it could've been worse, and she was grateful that Hunter could control himself. Peering over at him, Hunter drove stoically, with no expression to reveal how he currently felt. But Camilla didn't need a psychic to know, if the way he avoided eye contact with her was any indication.

"I can explain," Camilla began.

"Is he your husband?"

Hunter's voice matched his expression, posing the question with no emotion.

"No!" she huffed. "Of course not, what kind of woman do you think I am?"

Hunter chose not to answer that question.

"Steven's my ex."

"Ex-husband?"

"No!"

"Then why did he say it? Is he delusional? Did he escape from an insane asylum?"

"Is that a joke?"

"I'm not laughing," Hunter said. "A man comes out of nowhere and calls you his wife with no rebuttal on your part."

"How much did you hear?"

"Does it matter?"

Hunter made eye contact with her. Some of that iciness she'd seen back at WTZB was there, but it was fighting with another emotion; one that Camilla was certain she misread. Despair. But why would Hunter feel such a thing unless he loved her, and the thought of her being Steven's wife distressed him.

He pulled to the side of the road but didn't cut the engine.

"Look, I know our relationship is young, but you trust me at least, don't you?" She asked.

Hunter bit down on his jaw then blew out a deep breath.

"Tell me about him," he said, sitting against the seat.

Camilla gave Hunter a rundown about being engaged to Steven twice and the shenanigans he'd pulled.

"But he doesn't believe it's over. That's my fault. I shouldn't have taken him back the first time."

Hunter scoured her face. "Do you still love him?"

"In the sense that I don't want him to have a fatal accident, yes."

"That's not what I meant."

"Then no," she said plainly.

The vehicle became quiet as they watched one another.

"Take out a restraining order on him. I'll call Chief Fletcher and make sure it's adequately implemented."

"Let me talk to him first."

Hunter frowned. "To say what?"

"Just to let him know I mean business, and if he ever comes around again, I'm putting an order of protection out on him."

"That's not going to fly."

"Why not?"

"Do you think I care to sit back and wait for him to come around and manhandle you again? What happens if I'm not there, and he hurts you?"

There it was again. Despair. Camilla reached out and caressed his face.

"You really do care about me, don't you?"

"More than it makes sense."

Camilla's heart rocked against her chest, and a smile covered her lips. Hunter reached for her chin, and without much effort lured Camilla in for an impromptu kiss. When they parted, both hovered before drawing away completely.

"I'll make a deal with you," Hunter said.

"Okay."

"Take out the restraining order today, and I won't murder him the next time he shows up."

Camilla gasped. "Hunter!"

"What?"

"What kind of deal is that?"

"I thought it was a pretty good one."

Camilla huffed.

"So, what do you say?"

Camilla's stomach growled, and they both heard it. Hunter put the car in drive and pulled away from the corner. They headed in the direction of Louie's Steakhouse and Grill with Camilla never agreeing to Hunter's deal.

Chapter Twenty-Two

The week went on without another word from Steven. But Camilla knew she hadn't heard the last of him. The thing that made her more uncomfortable was now Steven knew she was dating Hunter, and his outburst at WTZB earlier that week was a bit disturbing. Steven was used to getting his way, so Camilla had never seen his ugly side, but Camilla replayed the way he yanked her, demanding she come with him. *Or else what?* That was the part that had Camilla checking corners every time she left her job and even at times when she was at the grocery store.

It was tiresome, and on top of that, she hadn't expressed these feelings to Hunter. Her reasoning was plain and simple. Hunter was not the type of man to sit idly by while his woman feared for her safety. He would most likely put Steven out of his misery. *Do you believe Hunter would really kill*

Steven? Her first response was to say no, but she couldn't be sure. Camilla sat inside her car that was parked in her assigned space at The Regency.

Tomorrow was Friday and she was going to meet Hunter's parents. She'd decided not to tell him they should wait, partly because of being distracted by her surroundings and relatively because a part of her wanted to meet Mr. and Mrs. Valentine. But still, Camilla sat in the parking lot, with her cell in hand thinking about sending Hunter a bland text about needing to postpone. Camilla bit down on her lip. Maybe she was just nervous. Instead of sending him that text, she sent him another.

Hey you. Do you mind if I bring along a friend to lunch tomorrow?

She hit send then waited patiently as her mind ran around the idea she had. It didn't take long for Hunter to respond. When her phone beeped, it brought an exhilarating smile to her face.

Just the woman I was thinking of. Is this friend Corinne?

The smile journeyed further.

No. You met her at the ribbon-cutting ceremony. My assignment editor, Allison Sullivan.

Send.

I don't see why not. Where are you?

Camilla texted back hurriedly.

Home.

Send.

When do you suppose I'll get to see this home you say you have? I'm starting to believe you don't

really live at The Regency, and you're a foreign spy sent to gain the heart of a wealthy bachelor in order to find out our governments secrets.

Camilla giggled and responded to his text.

I didn't know you had government secrets, but now that I do, you must tell me what they are since I've won your heart.

Camilla was only joking, but when her phone beeped again, the message took her breath away.

Damn it. I've always known a woman would be the end of me. I'm glad it was you, Angel.

She reread his words several times, and her heart rate increased. Could it be possible? That Camilla had stolen his heart? She reminisced back over the conversations they'd had throughout the week. Particularly the one during lunch on Wednesday.

"There is something I've wanted to ask you, but I'm not sure if you're up for discussing it." Camilla sat her fork down and rubbed her lips together. Her eyes fluttered over to Hunter, and he held them with a dynamic stare of his own.

"What's on your mind, Angel?"

Their table quieted as Camilla internally pushed herself to move forward, but something told her that what she wanted to know was a heavy subject for Hunter.

"Trevor," she said. Camilla examined his face. Hunter didn't seem to go still like he did the first time she mentioned Trevor. That gave her a bit of hope that Hunter had warmed up to her.

"What would you like to know?"

Hunter pulled his legs up from the relaxed languid position they were stretched out in to rest on his feet beneath the table. *So much for warming up.*

"I can tell this is a hard subject for you, and I completely understand if you'd rather not get into it."

"Ask me your question, Angel," he encouraged.

uHunHCamilla swallowed. "Okay, originally when I asked you said he was your brother, but you changed the subject pretty quickly so…"

Hunter's gaze traveled over her face. "He was, my brother." He cleared his throat, and his voice grew deeper. "He didn't make it."

She saw the solemnness in his eyes, and her heart broke for him.

"Remember when I told you we were born septuplets?"

"Yes."

"Trevor was among us. He lived for forty-five days in the NICU before he passed." Hunter didn't move as he spoke. "Unfortunately, he didn't get enough nutrition like the rest of us, and it caused him to have complications that overcame him."

"Hunter, I'm so sorry."

"Me, too, and you're right," he continued. "It's a hard subject. I always wonder what knowing my little brother would've been like. What kind of person he would've become, the things he would be invested in, and if I could kick his ass on the basketball court like I do the others."

Camilla smiled softly. Hunter was being a good sport trying to bring some light into the conversation.

"Sometimes, I think I see him in my dreams. He's never

quite clear to me, but I sense that he's there. Do you think that's crazy?"

"Of course not. I believe it's him."

Hunter's brows rose. "You do?"

"Sure. I believe in a higher power, and I know from my own personal experiences that God has his way of calming our spirits. May not be in the way we would like it to happen, but He is there nonetheless."

Hunter watched Camilla for a long moment. "You know I've never told anyone that. My brothers would crack on me, if I did." He smiled, but it was cut short.

"I don't believe that. I know your brothers might be like all brothers on their siblings, but when it comes to Trevor, they might surprise you. Who knows, it's possible that they've met him, too."

Hunter's heart swelled at the idea that Trevor was really visiting him and the possibility that his brothers had interacted with him as well. It gave Hunter the courage to talk to them about it, and right then and there, he knew more than anything that Camilla had been sent to him, too.

"Thank you, Angel. That means more to me than you know."

"Always," she said, and deciding to lighten the mood, she switched to another topic altogether. "Once upon a time, you asked me what was the one thing I'd long to do or have that I had yet to achieve," Camilla said. "So now I throw that question back at you. Tell me, Hunter, what does a man who appears to have everything want most in life?"

Hunter didn't bat an eye in thought. A smile curved up his lips then he spoke. "Children."

To say Camilla was taken by surprise was an understatement. "Children?"

Hunter nodded. "I've always wanted a house full of children. An entire football team with the cheerleaders to match."

A slightly horror-stricken look crossed Camilla's face, and it didn't slip by Hunter.

"Don't look so frightened, Angel. I take it by that look you don't want children?"

"Uh— well, it's not that I don't want them, uh…"

Hunter accessed her with a squinting peer and a thorough perusal.

"Don't worry about it for now. That comes later."

Camilla had been distracted the rest of their meal. Much like him, when she'd asked the question Camilla didn't expect that response. She almost regretted her inquiry and his comment about it coming later, what did that mean? Last week's sexcapade rewound in her mind. They hadn't used a condom in the heat of the moment, all five or six times throughout the night and in the shower the next morning. Camilla didn't know how to chastise herself. Being with Hunter felt perfect so although her actions were reckless, she didn't care.

Camilla cleared her throat and her mind long enough to send a text message to Allison.

Hey Allison, I know it's late, so I'll just cut right to the chase. Are you free for lunch tomorrow?

Send. It took about three full minutes before Allison responded.

It depends, are you asking me out on a date because I don't go both ways.

A burst of laughter shot from Camilla, and she shook her head in disbelief while her fingers tapped the screen in a dance.

Ha, ha, very funny. Actually, I'm having lunch with Hunter tomorrow at his parents' home, and I'm inviting you to come along. You know Lance will probably be there.

Mentioning Lance must have given Allison spirit fingers because this time she texted back within seconds.

You should've started the conversation with that. Count me in.

Camilla chuckled again.

Be ready at noon.

INSIDE HER APARTMENT, Camilla sat with her laptop open on the bed and her legs folded underneath her. As much as she wanted to go knock on Hunter's door and let him ravish her, she needed the rest, so she could feel and look her best tomorrow. Being with Hunter would just make her feel like sleeping the day away, so she opted to stay put.

As her eyes traveled over the screen, Camilla frowned. Throughout the week she'd been keeping up with news reports in Florida that said Hurricane Jasper was headed for the Keys. There were three potential paths Hurricane Jasper could take and two of them cut straight through her old neighborhood where her parents lived. The governor was already saying if Hurricane Jasper came close to hitting the mainland, as predicted, he would declare a state of emergency.

That was the one thing about the sunshine state. For as beautiful as it was, there was never a winter season that went by when a hurricane didn't threaten to wipe out the masses. Picking up her phone, Camilla dialed her parents. The phone rang twice before it was answered.

"Hello, baby, is everything all right?" Sharon Augustina asked with worry tones in her voice.

"Everything is fine, Mom, I'm sorry to call so late."

"Oh, you gave me quite a scare there." Sharon paused. "What has you up at 1 a.m.?"

"Hurricane Jasper."

"Oh, don't you go worrying about us, you know we've got the fallout shelter if we need to take cover."

"The fallout shelter won't hold against Hurricane Jasper. It's in need of serious updating, and this is a category five storm we're talking about."

"Yeah, well, we have a little time before finding out if it will hit us or not."

"Next weekend, Mother. Are you and Dad going to wait until it's on the mainland?"

"Where should we go?"

"Is that a serious question?"

"Listen, baby, your father and I don't want to intrude on what you've got going on in Chicago."

"Is that another serious statement?"

Sharon paused, and Camilla cut in. "Because I'm

certain if it were me, you would be very outspoken about me leaving."

Sharon sighed. "You're right. I'll talk to your father."

"No, I'll talk to him."

He's sleeping right now, and you know he gets grumpy if you wake him up, and he hasn't had his eight hours."

"I don't need to talk to him right now. I'm taking a trip down there, and both of you are coming back with me. Corinne doesn't know it yet, but so is she."

"Oh, baby."

"It'll be Monday. I have a few things this weekend to take care of but when I get there, you might as well have your bags packed."

"You know your father will never be swayed into leaving."

"He will if it's me swaying him. Daddy never could refuse his little girl, so I'll put it on thick if I need to. You just have the bags packed and ready."

Sharon chuckled a bit. "I will."

"Thank you, Momma."

"I love you, baby. Get some rest. Makes no sense worrying about something that's happening in the future, tonight."

"I'm going now. Good night, Momma. Love you, too."

They ended the call, and Camilla thought about calling to threaten Corinne with being kidnapped if she refused to leave. But the thought didn't last long; instead, it switched to Hunter and the many times he'd stolen her breath with a solitary kiss. She was in a relationship for fifteen years and never had she felt so treasured and taken care of like with Hunter. What did that say about Steven? Camilla wasn't sure if that meant he sucked that bad or if the two of them were never meant to be. Because in the timeframe Camilla had been with Hunter, she'd quietly fell in love with him. His gentle caresses at times were soothing, and when he became a fierce lover, it was all-consuming. The intellect he bestowed was almost sexier than when he stared her down with a smoldering gaze. Almost.

Camilla closed her laptop and rolled to her belly, stuffing her face into the pillow, and before another thought took root, she was sleeping like a baby.

Chapter Twenty-Three

"*I*'m glad I re-thought the first outfit I changed into," Allison said.

Camilla glanced at her friend as she followed the GPS to Hunter's parent's estate. "What did you have on at first?"

"An off the shoulder sweater dress. It stopped mid-thigh and looked a little hoochie." Allison scanned Camilla's attire. "That was the right move considering you're over here dressed like FLOTUS."

Camilla cracked a smile. "I'll take that as a compliment."

"You should."

With her hair neatly slicked back and pinned on top of her head, Camilla sat in the passenger seat with her legs crossed in a black knee length long sleeved dress. It hugged her waist and flared over her hips, keeping her curves hidden and giving her a Mary Poppins look. Her jewelry was light and simple, wearing diamond studded earrings, a thin 10 karat gold necklace with a small diamond that sat as a charm. There were no rings on her fingers, and her arms held a shea butter glow as if she'd moisturized in it.

"You may want to put your coat back on. We're coming up to our destination."

There was a hint of excitement and fear in Allison's voice. Camilla looked her over. "You're not nervous, are you?"

Allison peered at Camilla then quickly took her eyes back to the road. "Yes, I am nervous. Unlike you, this will be my first time meeting Lance, and if he's as gorgeous in person as he is in pictures and on TV, stick a fork in me, I'm done."

Camilla laughed as the GPS informed them their destination was on the right. Both ladies took their attention to the large castle-like estate.

"My God in Heaven," Allison said, clutching her pearls. "Who lives in this place?"

"Apparently, Hunter's parents do."

"Do you think they all lived here at some point?"

"Hmm, maybe. Let's go find out."

Allison pulled into the circular driveway then parked, and both ladies checked themselves once more then left the car for the front door. Allison reached to ring the doorbell when Camilla grabbed her hand.

Allison looked sharply over at her. "What?"

"Listen," Camilla said, putting her finger up to her lips in a hush. Allison and Camilla held perfectly still and laughter from the side of the home drift toward them. Allison frowned.

"What would they be doing outside as cold as it is?"

Instead of answering, Camilla left the porch and headed toward the voices. Allison scurried to catch up with her, and the closer they became, the more they could make out voices. One definitely belonged to Hunter, and the others were unknown. They passed several rose bushes outside as they traipsed over a manicured lawn. Camilla wondered how the bushes were blooming when the weather was still frigid.

They cut up to a brick pathway that announced their attendance from the click of their heels. Hunter was in a mid-air leap with a basketball rotating off the tip of his fingers. He came down hard, slamming the ball through the net. It swished as he dropped to his feet. His chest was bare, his shoulders broad and strong with melanin popping skin that shined as if he had moisturized in butter himself.

"Damn," Allison said. She shut her mouth tight after saying it, realizing just then that they were within hearing distance.

Three pairs of eyes turned their way. Lance, Hunter, and Xavier Valentine. Neither of the men wore a shirt but they were all in sweatpants. Hunter's gray, Xavier's navy blue, and Lance's maroon. A smile so strong it could light the city spread across Hunter's face.

"Hey, gorgeous," he said, walking away from the bouncing ball. He strolled up to Camilla and eased his strong arms around her waist. Glancing over at Allison, he nodded as a signature salute.

"What are you doing outside like this?" Camilla asked. "You're going to catch pneumonia."

Hunter's smile broadened, and his structured manly jaw only highlighted the grin.

"You think this is funny?"

"Nah, I just like it when you act as if you care about me."

Camilla put her hands on her hips. "Who says I'm acting? I do care about you. Is that what you think, that I'm playing a role?"

Hunter licked his bottom lip, and his eyes dropped to hers. "No, ma'am."

Exasperated, Camilla peered at him, and she wondered if this was one of those games he played just to see how much she did care about him.

"Are you messing with me?"

"Yeah."

Camilla rolled her eyes.

"Get used to it."

"Maybe I don't want to get used to it."

"But I like messing with you."

Camilla pursed her lips, and Hunter sank his mouth into hers. She thawed immediately, the frigid weather around them no longer a factor.

"Ahem," Allison said, clearing her throat. She still couldn't believe Camilla was dating Hunter. After all the "you're overreacting" speeches Camilla had given her, now they were actually a couple. And from the looks of things, hot and heavy in love. She wondered if they knew it yet and decided this time she would mind her business. Especially since, she only had a limited spell with Lance. She took her eyes to him, not mistaking him for Xavier.

Although there had been no introduction, Allison knew the chocolate bar with braided locks now standing with the ball in his hands was Lance.

"Hello," Allison said, taking the initiative.

"Why hello. What's your name, beauty?"

Allison's cheeks stung with heat at his compliment.

"I'm Allison Sullivan." She held her hand out, and Lance approached her, crushing the ball against his waist.

He held out his free hand, and a kernel of electricity spread through their fingers the moment they touched. Its sting made them lock eyes, and a smirk of a smile tinted Allison's lips.

"That's a lovely name. Welcome to our childhood home, Allison. I was trying to show my brother here who's got more game."

Xavier guffawed behind Lance as he sat perched on a wooden bench.

"You shouldn't tell the lady lies if you mean to make a good impression, young one," Hunter said. Hunter glanced to Allison. "In all actuality, I was putting a merciful beat down on him. You caught the end of it when you strolled up."

"That was one dunk," Lance defended. Xavier laughed with a deeper guffaw.

A screen door to the back entry rocked against the frame. Seconds passed when a voice rang out.

"You all come on in now. It's cold out here and lunch is ready."

The men turned to their mother's voice, and the women followed their gaze. When Mrs. Valentine spotted Camilla wrapped in Hunter's embrace, a gleam in her eyes sparkled, and the warm sensation made Camilla breathe a bit easier. Mrs. Valentine had an apron around her waist, a long-sleeve sweater that was rolled to her elbows, and skinny jeans fashioned on her legs. Mrs. Valentine's eyes traveled to Allison, standing mere inches in front of Lance. That only seemed to further lighten her brown eyes.

"I didn't know our company had arrived," her voice sang.

"We were coming right in," Hunter said. He looked back at Camilla. "You ready?" He released her long enough to step to her side and drape an arm around her shoulder.

"Yes."

Hunter pressed a kiss against her forehead, and they strolled up to Mrs. Valentine. "Mother, this is Camilla Augustina."

"How are you?" Camilla said, sticking her hands in Mrs. Valentine's before Hunter could finish the introduction.

"I'm fine, dear, and so happy to finally meet you."

Camilla peered at Hunter then took her eyes back to Mrs. Valentine. "Finally?" she asked.

A warm smile eased across Mrs. Valentine's face. With their hands still connected, Mrs. Valentine pulled Camilla forward and intertwined her arm in Camilla's, taking her completely away from Hunter.

"We can talk about that inside," Mrs. Valentine said, patting her hand.

They strolled toward the entry with the others in tow to

settle in for what would be an elaborate lunch and conversation.

ELABORATE WAS an understatement when describing the spread of food on the dining room table.

"This house is huge," Allison said in a whisper as she leaned close to Camilla's ear so only she could hear.

"I noticed and usually I'm not greedy, but this finger food looks so good my mouth is watering."

Allison chuckled as she and Camilla admired the display of food. Chopped steak and cheese spiraled into a sliced oven baked bread sat next to mini chicken salad sandwiches. Deviled eggs, and tuna stuffed mini romaine tomatoes were in line moving down the table. Beside them were fresh sushi rolls and grilled eggplant rollups with ricotta pesto. Apple slices, grapes, strawberries, and cherries sat in a crystal mini fruit cup with a whip cream topping in a swirl.

"I take it by that glazed look in your eye, the food is appealing to you?"

Camilla turned to Mrs. Valentine. "It all looks so delicious." Camilla noted the apron on Mrs. Valentine. She'd seen it outside, but now her interest was more piqued. "Did you cook this yourself?"

The gracious smile on Mrs. Valentine's face was beaming. "I did."

"Wow," both Camilla and Allison said.

"If you'd like to have a seat, my boys will serve you ladies."

Camilla's and Allison's brows rose, and they turned to look at the men who stood in a solid formation with hands behind their backs and aprons now around their waists. The bare chests they'd displayed outside had been covered in dark T-shirts and a lingering smirk sat in the corner of Hunter's lips.

"Oh, sure thing," Camilla said. She strolled to a seat at the extended dining table, and before she could sit, Hunter was there adjusting her chair. Camilla's eyes rode his thick arms and toned biceps and tried with strength not to ogle him in front of Mrs. Valentine. The smirk was still on his mouth, and a longing of some kind was trapped in his gaze.

"For you," he said in an offer for her to get comfortable.

"Thank you." Camilla's hand slipped down his shoulder, giving Hunter a light squeeze. She took her seat but hadn't missed the buzz crawling through the center of her palm from their brief touch.

After readjusting her chair, Hunter returned to the lunch spread and added a little bit of everything that Mrs. Valentine had to offer to Camilla's plate. Xavier, and Lance followed suit, with Lance fixing Allison plate, and Xavier his mother's. As the women waited for their lunch at the table, Camilla took a sip of her water to try and quench the sudden thirst she had, but it didn't seem to do much good. She lifted the glass to her lips again when Mrs. Valentine's crossed her legs at the ankles and linked her fingers.

"So, which one of you are going to give me grandbabies first," she asked.

A spray of water flew from Camilla's lips, and horrified, she covered her mouth and choked back the rest.

"Oh, dear, are you all right?" Mrs. Valentine asked, handing a crispy folded napkin to Camilla.

Hurriedly, Camilla dabbed her mouth and wiped down her hand and the splotches on her dress.

"Mother, you don't start off a conversation with who's going to give you grandbabies," Hunter said.

Xavier laughed, but Lance dropped his head and grimaced. He didn't even know Allison. Why would his mother be so desperate for grandchildren that she would ask her that?

"Well what should I start with? I already know her."

Camilla was taken aback by that comment.

"How do you know her when you've just met her, Ma?" Lance's easy-grooving voice asked.

"Well, I don't know Allison, yet, but there's only a matter of time for that. I know Camilla. Hunter talks about her all the time."

Camilla curved her head to glance up at Hunter who stood next to her holding a plate. He sat it down in front of her and rested a warm palm on her shoulder.

"Forgive my mother, she anxiously wants grandchildren and thinks she knows you through the few conversations we've had."

"Few?" Mrs. Valentine said. She eyed Camilla. "I've talked to my son four times this week, and in each conversation, he's brought you up. And to be truthful, I didn't say anything about grandbabies then. He adores the softness in your eyes, your humanitarian character, and your beautiful smile."

"Mother," Hunter said.

Mrs. Valentine ignored him and leaned in to whisper, but everyone still heard her as they were all tuned in to the conversation. "You make life easy for him. Even when he's having an odd day at VFC Energy, it doesn't agitate him the way it used to do. You make him whole, Camilla, nothing ruins his day anymore because he looks forward to getting home to you." Mrs. Valentine peered at Hunter then went back to Camilla. "He told me as much. I'm not making this up."

Xavier whistled. "At least I know now to tell Dad if this ever happens to me," he said.

Mrs. Valentine glanced at her son. "Why, your father will just tell me. None of you can hide this type of information from your mother. So just hush."

"Speaking of my father, where is he?" Hunter asked, trying to change the subject.

"He's at a golf tournament, so you'll just have to deal with me for now." Mrs. Valentine put a wide smile on her face. "Now, where was I?"

Chapter Twenty-Four

Hunter and Camilla stood in the foyer of his parents' home with no words between them. Camilla shifted her weight, giving one foot more pressure than the other. She cleared her throat and licked her bottom lip. Mrs. Valentine had spilled all the beans, and she wondered what to make of the sudden information. Hunter had clearly poured out his heart to his mom, but he had yet to do it to her, so what gives?

"If you're ready to run for the hills," Hunter said, "forget about it. I can't let you go now."

Camilla's eyes jumped in surprise, and a smile, then a giggle eased from her mouth. Hunter stepped closer. "Please accept my apologies for my mother. She can be a bit over-bearing at times."

Camilla swallowed. "Well, if I ever need to know how you feel, I'll just call her and find out," she half-joked.

Hunter grinned, but it didn't lift his face. "You won't need to call her. I'll make sure to tell you myself."

"When do you think that'll start happening?"

"On the level that I've informed my mother, now. It happens from here forth." He exhaled a rushing wind of breath. "Camilla, I've never been with a woman like you before. One that is caring, strong-minded, intelligent, self-sufficient, beautiful, and invigorating." He reached out to caress her chin. "You're everything I've never had, and I'd like for you to stick around if you don't mind."

Camilla blushed, and her heartbeat rocked. "I feel the same way, Hunter." She exhaled an easy breath. "I've got to be honest, when I first met you, I judged you by the headlines and whispers I'd heard about the infamous Hunter Valentine."

"Those things are never true," he teased.

Camilla giggled. "Sure," she said, her voice soft and smooth. "What I've come to find is a charismatic, strong, professional, very handsome guy, and being with you has awakened parts of me I've never known, sexually or intellectually." A slow grin spread his lips. "And I'd love to stick around," she finished.

Hunter gripped her chin and pulled her to his crushing mouth that sealed against her lips in a rapture of passion. A shield of rippling warmth poured over them, and Camilla quivered as their arms tied around one another.

"Mmmm," Camilla moaned, and in that moment, she couldn't find a care to give about making out in his parents' home. Their tongues mixed as a pleasurable wave ran the course of their limbs, festering a plantation of springing nerves on their skin.

When they slowed, it was Hunter who spoke first.

"I'd love to take this back to my place, but there is something I want to show you first."

Camilla kissed his sweet lips again. "Okay, when do we leave?"

Hunter's hand slipped down her arm, his fingers linking with hers. "We go now," he said.

The two didn't waste time saying their goodbyes, and Allison didn't mind being left behind. She wasn't done with Lance yet anyway, that much was obvious as the two sat so close in the family room you'd think at any second Allison would be in his lap.

Inside the Maserati, Hunter powered the sports vehicle and pulled out of the estate, heading uptown to a venue he'd rented out.

"Are you going to tell me where we're going?"

"No."

"How did I know you were going to say that?"

Hunter chuckled. "Because you know me now."

They held smiles on one another as the statement rang with some truth. There was always much to be discovered between the both of them, but they were confident enough with the information they had.

The sports vehicle turned into an underground parking garage and Hunter parked next to a set of double doors. They slipped out, and Camilla strolled to the trunk as Hunter lifted it and pulled out a bag.

"You've been shopping?" she asked, staring at the Old Navy bag.

"I needed to pick a few things up we'll need for where we're going."

"I can't believe you went inside Old Navy without causing a riot."

Hunter laughed. "I didn't. I sent my assistant."

"Ah ha, that makes more sense."

Hunter closed the hood and dropped the keys into his pocket then grabbed Camilla's hand.

"Let's go."

The double doors opened as they approached, and they walked through two more sets of doors before coming to a huge open space. Camilla gasped and looked over at Hunter in surprise.

"Oh my God!" she screeched with laughter cruising from her throat. In front of her was a wall that rose so high Camilla had to take a step back just to follow it to the top. Whipping her head around, she stared at him. "Rock climbing!?"

"You see, Angel, the way I perceive it is, if you're going to climb a mountain, you should probably practice first. This wall is two hundred and forty-one feet high. It's the tallest in the world from my research. Mount Everest is staggering twenty-nine thousand feet high. This wall doesn't come close to that, but if you're going to climb like a pro, you've got to start somewhere."

Camilla laughed hard and slinked into his chest, wrapping her arms around him. Hunter's embrace was soft, warm and stimulating, and the bag in his hand bumped her butt.

"How did you know I wouldn't come dressed to climb a wall," she asked, thinking about the bag in his hand.

"I didn't, but I like to be prepared. I always take the initiative."

That was something Camilla had noticed as well. An instructor traipsed toward them. "Good evening, Mr. Valentine."

Camilla pulled from Hunter's strong hold and turned to the guide.

"You must be Ms. Camilla Augustina," the instructor said.

"Yes," Camilla responded with a smile in her voice.

"It's nice to meet you. I hear you're into climbing."

Camilla giggled. "You could say that." She slipped a hand up Hunter's chest.

"If you follow me, I'll show you to the changing room, then we can get started."

They moved through the building with Camilla gaping at the huge wall. They changed, and the instructor helped them correctly secure their equipment then they got started. Hunter stood behind Camilla as she perched a foot on one of the wall's rocks and reached to grab the other. His gaze combed over the back of her thighs as her legs stretched and her ass puckered toward him. Hunter wasn't trying to gape at her, but he was a man, one who wanted Camilla every moment of the day. He saw himself move forward and bite down a mouth full of ass and had to internally calm his carnal urge for the sake of becoming a cave man.

Camilla moved up the wall with structured strength and a bit of agility. It turned Hunter on to watch her ascend, and if he hadn't figured it before right then, Camilla became his queen. She paused for a second, and Hunter thought she fought to hold her grip. But in reality, she was looking for him, and when she didn't see him beside her, Camilla glanced down.

"Are you going to stand there and watch me, or are you coming up?"

"I'm not sure. The view of you from here has me awestruck."

Camilla laughed. "Come up, baby, I need you."

She didn't have to tell him twice. Hunter climbed the wall with the tenacity of a skilled mountaineer with muscles bulging with each stretch of his limbs. When he reached her, instead of pausing on either side of Camilla, he paused on top of her. With each of his legs meeting the rock right beneath her foot. His closeness came with a pocket of heat that padded over Camilla's skin in a rushing landslide.

"You were saying you needed me," his intoxicating voice drummed. "How's this? Too close, or?"

Camilla pulled in a slow breath then tossed a glance over her shoulder to meet up with his punching gaze. "Perfect," she said almost in a purr, and there on the wall, they kissed with a passionate fervor that sent a flame shooting through them both. Hunter's dick hardened, and the extensive limb pushed against her derriere, causing Camilla to moan in return.

When their lips parted, Hunter gave a massive effort to

calm himself, but it failed. "If you want to get to the top," he said his voice raspy, "then we should probably keep going."

In a brazen move, Camilla managed to twist herself in a way where she released the rock in her hand then held on to his shoulder and instead of her toes piercing the rock below, now, the heel of her foot did as she faced Hunter. His eyes dimmed at her bravery.

"I want to get to the top," her sultry voice pulled. "But not of this wall."

Her implication was blatant, and Hunter gave her fair warning.

"This is going to be a wild ride to the bottom, you may want to hold on."

Camilla's face lit up with a smile, and quickly, she tossed her arms around his neck. Hunter let go of the wall just as his thick arms of muscle roped around her waist. She screamed as he pushed off the giant rock and they descended to the ground. The harness they wore made them spring, up and down, back and forth in a twirl, and Camilla laughed up a storm of giggles as the thrill tickled every bone inside of her. When they finally regained their bearings, Camilla propped against him, and they kissed. It took them all of ten minutes to change and leave the under-ground dome. In no time, they were back at The Regency, and the entire ride had been revitalizing with Camilla reaching into Hunter's lap and grabbing a handful of his dick.

She stroked him all the way there, which was probably how they arrived so quickly. Inside the elevator, she jumped into his arms, and they sucked in each other's mouths, completely taken. When the door dinged, and Hunter stepped out, Camilla pulled her mouth away slowly.

"I was thinking," she said. "Would you like to come to my place this time?"

Hunter stopped walking, and a mischievous smile lit up his lips. "I have the privilege of seeing your spot now?"

Camilla laughed. "Mmhmm," she said.

"Well shit, woman, I thought you'd never ask."

Camilla giggled as Hunter stepped back into the elevator with Camilla still wrapped around him.

"Wait," she said, "where are you going?"

"You said—"

"I know." She gave him a coy look. "I live on this floor."

Hunter's brows furrowed. "Angel, there's only one other apartment on this floor, and—"

"It belongs to me," she said, finishing his sentence.

"Bullshit."

Camilla nudged her nose into his neck to hide her smirking face.

"Give me your key," Hunter said. "I don't believe you."

Aghast, Camilla pulled back from him. "Oh, now you don't believe me?"

"Hell no. There's no way you've been sleeping seconds from me without my knowledge."

"All right."

Camilla wiggled out of his hands and jumped to her feet. She gripped his palm and pulled him back off the elevator and sauntered up to the door. Digging in her purse, Camilla removed her key and stuck it in the lock. Hunter watched closely to see if it would turn or if she would back out at the last minute.

Her hand jiggled, and the lock clicked. She pushed the door, and it swung open. She sashayed inside then pivoted around and held out her arms as his mouth dropped.

"Tada!" she said.

"Son of a bitch," he swore.

Camilla giggled. "Hey!"

"I'm not calling you a son of a bitch, I'm just..."

Camilla chuckled. "I guess."

"I knew it."

"Knew what?

"This whole time you were an international spy."

Camilla fell out in a heap of giggles, and Hunter scooped her up, shutting the door simultaneously with his foot.

"Ah!" she screamed as he bit down on her neck and walked dominantly to the master bath.

They were stripped and inside the heated shower within seconds, clawing at each other in nefarious mating calls. She was in his arms when Hunter entered her vagina, driving into her folds with deep diving plunges. He gripped her butt cheeks in his palms, spreading them as he propelled inside her.

"Oh!" she moaned out. Her arms were tied around his mountainous shoulders as Hunter plunged in and out of her heated core. "Fuck!" She screamed. And that's exactly what they did.

Hunter's mouth sank against her throat, where he sucked her while blasting Camilla with temerarious strokes.

"Ah!"

She clung to him, wrapped in desire that tingled her body and ignited her skin. She tightened her pussy muscles, and it didn't slow his thrusts but only propelled him into overdrive.

"Oh my God! Oh my God! Hunter!"

He turned from the spray of water then pushed her back into the shower wall and fucked her so unremitting and barbaric she shouted one languorous scream.

"I want you to come all over this dick, Angel," he said. "Have my babies," he prodded.

"Ah! Oooh!" she screamed.

"Say you will."

He folded Camilla, pushing her legs so far, her knees met the wall. His hands braced against the back of her thighs and Hunter rocked into her pussy on a dangerous excursion.

"Tell me," he demanded.

"Fuck! Fuck! Fuck!" she screamed.

"Tell me," he said again, driving into her as echoing sounds of penetration flooded the shower stall.

"Please, Hunter!"

Camilla's eyes crossed, and her mouth was caught in an O. Hunter became a savage, driving into her so hard, and expeditiously Camilla's thighs went numb. They dissipated, moving against each other until their bones liquefied.

"Tell me," he growled sucking in a mouthful of her nipples simultaneously.

"Yes! Yes! Fuck yes, I'll have your babies!"

Her toes curled, and she shouted as his plunging thrusts

tore into her womb with the blunt force of an electric hammer. Hunter lifted his mouth on a curse then sucked her nipples in again just as his orgasm found momentum.

"I'm going to come so fucking hard!" Camilla shouted.

And Hunter clapped into her steadfast like the beat of sticks to a drum. They sang out, with profanity leaving both of their lips as they released together. They were sealed, and their mouths crushed hungrily as their cream interspersed. A euphoric jolt crawled around them, and they were lost in the glow of love.

Hunter's chest rose and fell along with Camilla's, then reluctantly, he removed his mouth from hers but kept her eye on his.

"Say you meant it," he said.

She knew instantly what he referenced.

"Hunter..."

He stared, waiting for her refusal.

"I meant it," she said, and his heartbeat knocked inside his chest.

"Angel, please don't play with me."

"I'm not," she said. "I don't know how to explain it, Hunter, but all I want is you and whatever you want. But..." she added, "we have to be 50/50 parents because I'm not taking care of a whole kid by myself."

He laughed a deep rumbling guffaw, then took hold of her lips and intermixed his tongue with her own. Another moan rooted from Camilla, and before they had a chance to pull apart again, they were rocking once more against the wall.

Chapter Twenty-Five

*I*t was like a dream, one that she never wanted to wake from. Camilla strolled out of The Regency with a small rollaway suitcase on wheels. Robert the valet approached her.

"Good morning, can I get your car, Ms. Augustina?"

"Yes, thank you, Robert." She handed him her keys.

"My pleasure," he said, strolling away to retrieve her rental.

Camilla stood in a semi-daze. It was Monday morning, and everything about the weekend had been right. Not only had she spent it relaxing without a care in the world, but the man she'd been with had gotten into her system so much that Camilla had a secret confession with herself. She was in love with Hunter. He'd been nothing but the best, and Camilla almost couldn't believe her luck. When she informed him she was flying to Florida to drag her parents back to Chicago, he understood, though he wasn't too happy.

Reports of Hurricane Jasper had not let up, and he'd not asked but told Camilla, to get back before Wednesday.

"If you're not back by 8 a.m. Wednesday morning, I'm catching the first flight out to Florida."

"To do what exactly? If I'm not back by then, it'll be because I haven't convinced my hardheaded father to come along."

"I'll drag you and your daddy back, it doesn't make me any difference."

Camilla's mouth had dropped, and she gasped. "You can't drag my father back. He's as big as you!"

Hunter peered at her.

"Well," she backtracked, "he runs a close third, anyway," she said, waving her hand. "My father's a grown man. You can't."

"I can, and I will."

Camilla pursed her lips with a smirk, enjoying his protectiveness while pretending to be offended.

"Did you take the order of protection out on Steven?"

Camilla couldn't fix her face to tell a lie, and she didn't want to. "Not yet."

Hunter didn't respond but kept a scrutinized gaze on her.

"I'm doing it Monday before I head to the airport."

"Thank you," he said.

So here she was on her way to the police station then off to Chicago O'Hare. A car exited the garage and pulled in front of the entrance. Camilla's eyes glanced to the driver. It was

Robert. She frowned then her eyes widened, and her mouth parted on a gasp. She took in the pink salmon Toyota Prius with sour apple chrome rims and her hand flew over her heart.

"Can't be," she whispered.

Robert exited the vehicle, leaving the door open. He motioned to the car. "Your Prius awaits, Ms. Augustina."

"Robert," she said, "there must be some mistake. I don't own—this isn't my car."

"Yes, it is," Robert said as a fact, "courtesy of Mr. Valentine."

She was stunned, and completely turned around. She released the handle on her luggage, and her hands flew to her mouth. She tiptoed to the car, and Robert took the initiative of putting her suitcase in the trunk while Camilla got a glimpse at its interior.

"Oh my God," her muffled voice said. "I can't believe this." Camilla trailed to the back of the vehicle, getting a look at the sour apple license plate. A bright smile covered her face, and she continued her perusal, strolling out into the street then around the fender.

"Congratulations," Robert said. "She's a beauty."

Still flabbergasted, Camilla slipped into the driver's seat and closed the door. She powered down the window and waved at Robert.

"Thank you!" she said.

"You're more than welcome, Ms. Augustina."

Camilla gazed around the interior and sat her cell phone in the clip perched on the dashboard.

"Siri, call Hunter."

"Calling Hunter."

The phone rang three times, and for a second, Camilla thought she would go to voicemail until his smooth baritone voice filled the line.

"Good morning, Angel."

"Good morning," she said with a smile in her voice. "Babe, did you buy me a car?"

There was silence on the line.

"Hunter?"

"I don't know what you're talking about."

"I can't believe you bought me a car!" Her smile was wide now, and she burst into a fit of animation. "I don't know if I can take this from you."

Camilla drove to the police station with Hunter on speakerphone.

"The car is in your name. You own it. So, if you don't want it, then you'll have to sell it."

Camilla gasped. "I could never do that!"

"Then keep it."

"But... but..." her mind whirled. She was excited but feeling nervous about accepting such a large gift. "Hunter..." she droned.

"Angel, I'm in the middle of a board meeting, but keeping the wheels is up to you. I won't feel bad if you give it away."

Camilla pursed her lips. "Like I'd ever do that, and I'm so sorry for interrupting, you should've let the call go to voicemail."

"Never."

Camilla blushed, and butterflies waved through her stomach.

"Well, I hope it goes well. Call me when you leave for the day."

"Have a safe flight and come home to me," he said.

Camilla blushed again. "I will."

The phone became quiet as they both relished in the love that bloomed inside them for one another.

"I'm missing you already," he said. "See you soon."

"Yeah, see you."

Camilla ended the call and squealed with a hard blush. Once again, she took her eyes around the vehicle then parked at the station and pulled herself together.

"Okay, Camilla, just go in and get this over with."

Much to her chagrin, Camilla left the brand-new Toyota Prius in the parking lot then went inside and filled out the necessary paperwork.

FOUR HOURS and forty minutes later Camilla arrived at Miami International Airport. She exited the aircraft still on a cloud from the wonderful surprise Hunter had given her. It wasn't until she heard a squeal, that Camilla snapped out of her fog and caught Corinne running toward her. The women did a tap dance around each other then pulled in for a hug.

Corinne took a good look at Camilla, and her mouth stayed open showing all thirty-two teeth in her mouth.

"What?" Camilla asked.

"Girl, look at you! It's only been what, two weeks, and Hunter's got you glowing and shit."

Camilla tossed her head back and laughed. "Shut up!"

"He does!"

Camilla glanced down at herself, unable to hide the beam on her face.

"She doesn't even deny it," Corinne stated. "You guys are hot together. Just wait until the media gets a hold of this."

"Oh my God, we've been doing such a good job keeping it under wraps."

"I can tell because it hasn't made it to TMZ yet. You guys are for sure hiding. Well come on, let's get out of here. Tell me about it on the way to brunch."

The women trailed out of the airport and got inside Allison's Mazda and made their way across town. The weather in Miami was unmistakably different than Chicago's, with humid temperatures—the state's signature for sunny weather.

"There was a bit of turbulence on the plane," Camilla said, taking note of the gloomy skies. "When I checked the weather, it said cloudy with a chance of rain. So then why does it look like the sky will fall at any moment?"

"Most times they get it right, but sometimes, they don't." Corinne shrugged, thinking nothing of it. "Where do you want to eat?"

"Let's go to Tongue and Cheek."

Corinne wiggled her brows with a smirk. "You're in the mood for chicken and waffles, huh?"

"More than you know."

"We're right around the corner."

"You must have known I'd want some."

"I knew you would want to be in the area your parents live."

Camilla nodded, and Corinne parked. They left the Mazda and found a seat inside, getting comfortable. Camilla lifted her nose to the air and moaned as she took a whiff of the hot food that lingered.

"Did you eat before you left?"

"I had a croissant and a cup of cappuccino for breakfast."

A server strolled to their table, and Camilla happily gave her order without looking at the menu.

"Make that a double," Corinne chimed, getting the chicken and waffles. Once the waitress sailed away to place their orders, Corrinne said, "So, tell me what's happened since I've been gone. It's felt like a lifetime."

"Corinne." Camilla sighed and glanced toward the windows in thought. The palm trees swayed as if a storm was brewing, but Camilla brought her focus back to the conversation. "Hunter is wonderful. I don't know if I should be scared or relieved that God has given me a second chance at this relationship thing."

"It's all right to be scared, girl. Trust me, when it comes to men, it's hard sometimes to believe you have a good one with countless bad apples in the bunch."

Camilla nodded. "Especially with the reputation Hunter has, but there is something else."

"What's up?"

"Is it possible to get pregnant within a few weeks? It takes longer before you know, right?"

Corinne's eyes bugged out, and a chill fled down her skin. "Oh my God!"

"Ssssh!" Camilla said, shushing her friend. "Can you answer my question first before you get all crazy?"

Corinne began to hyperventilate. "Okay." She blew out a deep breath. "Um, let me think about this."

Camilla nodded with a knot in her throat.

"Um, I don't know," Corinne answered.

Deflated, Camilla pushed out a long breath. "That's no help, Corinne."

"I know, I'm sorry, but tell me why do you think you may be pregnant? Have you taken a test?"

"No," she whined.

"Then why?"

"The first time we had sex we didn't use protection the entire night. And trust me, it was a long night."

Corinne nodded and smiled. "Okay, so when did you start using protection?"

Camilla avoided eye contact.

"Camilla?"

"We never did, okay?"

Another gasp fled from Corinne. "Damn, Camilla, you've never been this reckless."

"I knoooow, oh my God, what am I going to do! My cycle comes around every month on the same day like clock-work. I am not, nor have I ever been one of those girls whose cycle switches up. We've just entered a new month with no cycle in sight!" Camilla bit her fingertips. "And I can smell food."

Corinne frowned. "I can smell food, too, hell we're in a restaurant."

"No, I could smell the food before you pulled into the parking lot."

Corinne's eyes lurched, and she covered her mouth with one hand and sat back against her seat. "Oh my," she said.

"Corinne, you're scaring me to death!"

"Okay, this is what we'll do. Let's go to the dollar store and get you a pregnancy test."

Camilla nodded, and Corinne pushed her chair back and stood. Camilla reached across the table and grabbed her hand. "After we eat," she said.

A smirk crept across her lips, and Corinne reclaimed her chair. They ate their food in near silence with the hum of the restaurant's television in the background. Both were in their own thoughts—Corinne knowing Camilla wasn't a fan of kids and unable to detect how she would truly feel if she were pregnant. On the other side of the table, Camilla ate unhurriedly, as she wondered the same. Would she be excited, dreadful, or in despair? The thoughts almost drove her crazy until she couldn't take it anymore. With half of her meal still on her plate, Camilla sat her fork down and stood.

"Come on, you're barely touching your food anyway."

"Same as you," Corinne added. The ladies left money on the table and cleared the threshold. The door chimed as they left, and the winds seemed to be harsher outside.

"The meteorologist didn't say anything about harsh winds," Corinne mentioned.

They climbed into her car and drove to the nearest dollar store. Inside Camilla purchased the test then asked for a restroom.

"We don't usually let customers use the bathroom. It's for employees only," the clerk said. The woman glanced down at the test Camilla had just purchased. "However, because I feel this may be an emergency, I'll let you use it this time."

"Thank you so much," Camilla and Corinne chimed.

Inside the lavatory, Camilla paced back and forth, and she counted down the minutes it would take for the test to give her the necessary information.

"Come on, come on," she chanted. Camilla grabbed the examination and still there were no results. "Okay, calm down, Camilla, it's only been a few seconds." She paced again with the stick in her hand, but the blaring sound of an alarm commandeered her heartbeat, causing her to fly out of the bathroom.

"What's going on!?" She said, rushing down the aisle to Corinne.

Corinne, the manager, and associate, watched the news as a breaking report strolled across the screen. Hurricane Jasper was moving faster than the state of Florida had anticipated, and for all the people in Miami, it was time to take cover. A sharp gasp left Camilla.

"Oh my God!"

The alarm sailed throughout the town, and the manager grabbed Camilla by the arm.

"Come on, ladies, we've got to take shelter."

"No!" Camilla wiggled out of the manager's arm. "I've got to get to my parents!"

"There's no time, you'll be risking your life if you leave the building."

Corinne sucked in a deep breath. She'd known when her parents moved to Tennessee three years ago that she should've gone with them.

"Come on, if we're going, we're going now!"

Corinne and Camilla ran through the double doors, and the manager locked it behind them. The winds howled with ferocity as they jumped in the Mazda and fled down the boulevard in a blur. Camilla dialed her parents. Her mom answered on the first ring.

"Baby!" Her mother shrieked. "Thank God you're not here yet. Listen, don't come to Florida, it looks like this hurricane fooled us all because it's on its way. Don't worry about us, your father and I are taking refuge in the shelter."

"I am here!"

"What!?"

"I'm with Corinne, Mom, we're two minutes away from you!"

"Oh my God! Bernard! Bernaaard!" Her mother yelled. When her father approached, Camilla could hear him in the background.

"Camilla is here. She's on her way!"

"I'm pulling into the driveway, open the door."

Camilla removed the seat belt as Corinne skidded into the driveway of the two-bedroom art deco styled home. "They jumped out and ran to the door just as Bernard unbolted the lock with his wife standing idly by his side. Camilla ran into his arms, and Corinne followed.

"I wish you wouldn't have come," his thick voice boomed. Bernard glanced at the item in Camilla's hand, and realizing she was still holding the test, Camilla stuffed it into her back pocket without giving it a glance.

"I was trying to get you all out of here before this," she said. "The storm is a week early!"

"Come on, it's too late for that now."

Bernard locked the door, and the foursome went to the fallout shelter where they took cover from Hurricane Jasper.

Chapter Twenty-Six

*H*unter drove his Maserati down the boulevard with his mind in a daze about the princess cut diamond he'd just had handcrafted by his jeweler. His phone rang, pulling him from a trance, and he turned a corner and answered through his Bluetooth.

"Hunter," he said.

"He's on the move. Looks like he's headed to The Regency."

"Where are you?"

"Following him closely."

"Stay on him, I'm on my way."

Hunter ended the call and made a U-turn then dialed Camilla. He hadn't heard her voice since they'd spoken that morning, and it was now six in the evening. Hunter tried not to bother her, knowing she would be crowded with family and friends during her return. But Hunter couldn't help himself. He longed for Camilla as if he was in need of a breath of fresh air that eluded him whenever he inhaled. He hit send and waited a beat, but his call went straight to voicemail.

Hunter grimaced and redialed her but only ended up with the same result. He pushed out a rough breath then decided to let her be. It was probably a long day for her, maybe her phone needed charging. Riding up to The Regency, Hunter's grimace turned into a full-on scowl when seeing Steven approach The Regency doors. Since the day of their scuffle, Hunter had kept a detective on Steven, knowing at any time he would discover a way to find Camilla. Steven spoke to Robert who looked at Steven questionably as he watched him walk confidently through the rotating doors.

Hunter pulled up and parked then hopped out of the sports car.

"Two minutes," he said to Robert who approached for Hunter's keys to park the Maserati. With ease, Hunter moved through the door, and immediately, his eyes fixed on Steven.

Steven stood perched at the receptionist's desk trying to get information on Camilla's address. As Hunter approached, he could hear Steven talking to the woman.

"Camilla Augustina," he said. "I'm her fiancé, just came in town and wanted to surprise her," he lied.

Hunter slipped his hands into his pocket and leaned a shoulder into the counter. Steven glanced over at him, and recognizing him, instantly cursed.

Hunter nodded. "Yeah, that's right."

"This man is harassing me," Steven said, turning quickly back to the receptionist. "Call the police, please."

The receptionist glanced over at Hunter, and he winked with a smile. The woman returned his warm greeting and took a tiresome eye back to Steven. She didn't even know Steven, but knew in that moment, he was full of shit.

"Sir, this man lives in this building. So, if he is harassing you by being here, it would probably be best for you to leave."

Steven let out a harsh breath. "You've got to be kidding me."

"I'm afraid I'm not," the woman said.

Hunter chuckled. "You just couldn't help yourself, could you?" he said. "If it's any consolation I understand. My Camilla is a beautiful, intelligent, strong-willed woman. If I were you, I wouldn't want to lose her to the likes of a brother like me either. Because here's what's going to happen. I'm going to put a ring on her finger, and when I do, I won't call off the wedding because I'm not foolish enough to let go of a catch like her." An easy grooving laugh trekked from Hunter's mouth. It was as if Hunter could see visible steam coming out of Steven's ears.

"And trust me when I say, she will never want you again. I'm all she needs, now and forever more. Oh, and didn't you know, you're violating an order of protection."

Steven frowned, and he shortened her name when he spoke, "Camille doesn't have it in her to do something like that. Not with me. I'm in her heart more than she's willing to admit right now, but I know the feelings are mutual. That's what decades of love does to you."

"Hmmm, that's such a shame that you would think so little of Camilla. But it seems like with decades of *love*, as you call it, you still have no clue who she is."

Hunter glanced over at a tall dark skin man approaching with shades across his face and a badge on his hip.

"Let me introduce you to a friend of mine. This is Detective Shaw." Hunter held his hand out toward the detective, and Detective Shaw handed Hunter a piece of paper to which Hunter offered over to Steven.

Steven looked down at it like it was a snake then snatched the paper out of his hand.

"This is your order of protection, and you're violating it." Hunter glanced to Detective Shaw. "Detective."

Detective Shaw grabbed Steven by the arm. "Hey, get your hands off me!"

"I promise if you want to make a show in this lobby I'm all for it," Detective Shaw said.

Steven stared at the paper in disbelief, and with slow hesitancy, followed Detective Shaw to the exit.

"I'll be in touch," Detective Shaw said back to Hunter as he and Steven disappeared out of the building.

HUNTER HAD CALLED her several times and still his call went to voicemail. Now, he was worried. Surely, Camilla wouldn't leave her phone off this long. Hunter regretted not getting her parents' phone number, but he could seek it out if need be. He was so busy making sure he had their address because he planned to make good on his threat to come down if Camilla hadn't returned before Hurricane Jasper arrived. It was ten o'clock at night, and his mind had been so busy with getting her on the phone, Hunter had failed to turn on the news. His phone rang, and he answered immediately.

"Hunter," he said.

"Hey, brother, are you busy?" The voice belonged to Xavier.

"No, what's up?"

"I just knew you were going to tell me you were with Camilla."

"Why is that?"

"Because you two are inseparable. I was sure you were pussy whipped by now."

"Damn straight I am and fuck you all the same."

Xavier balled over in laughter.

"Camilla's not here. She went down to Florida to bring her parents back before the big storm hit."

Xavier's laughter was doused immediately. "You're not talking about Hurricane Jasper, are you?"

"That's the only storm coming through the Keys, isn't it?"

A string of profanity left Xavier's lips.

"What?" Hunter's thick voice drummed with anxiety.

"Brother, Hurricane Jasper hit earlier today. The weather forecasters got it wrong. Florida's been on emergency evacuation since around three."

Hunter's heart leaped in his chest, and he stood to his feet.

"Don't bullshit me, Xavier!" He roared.

"Man, I know how much you're into her. I wouldn't play with you on this."

Instantly, Hunter's soul felt crushed. He'd just met and fallen in love with the woman he planned to marry and raise a family with. It would be a sick joke to lose her before their life could even begin. A plethora of emotions swept through him; pain ricocheted through his chest and weakness tried to cripple him. He almost fell to his knees, but Camilla needed his help, and come hell or Mount Everest, Hunter was going to get her.

"Power up the jet," he said. "We're going to Florida."

Chapter Twenty-Seven

he Boeing 747 VIP private jet was halfway to Florida when it came upon heavy turbulence.

"You know you're one crazy SOB, right?"

Hunter turned to Xavier.

"What does that make you?"

"Same," Xavier said. "For all the trouble you're going through, you better love this girl."

"I do."

Xavier stared at his brother.

"And she's going to be my wife."

Xavier's brows arched. He wanted to call Hunter out on a lie but considering their current situation it was thoroughly possible that he was telling the truth.

"Wait, how long have you known her?"

"Long enough."

Hunter waited for another rebuttal, but Xavier gave

none. The aircraft hit another patch of hard turbulence, and the pilot came across the loudspeakers.

"We're going to land now. Our current location is Hialeah, Florida. It's about twenty-five minutes to Miami by car. This is as close as I can get you without killing us all."

Xavier cursed a million times and cut his eyes at Hunter. "I better be the best man," he said.

Hunter smirked. "Deal."

They buckled their seats and prepared for a not-so-smooth landing. The cabin shook, and they said a silent prayer as the jet fought the winds to get to the ground. It was a rough twenty-minute descent, but once there, the pilot came over the speaker again.

"We will have to stay put until the storm passes. Good luck, Hunter."

Hunter unbuckled his belt and stood to his feet. With persistence, he pulled on an overhead coat and left the Boeing 747 with Xavier right behind him.

"Where are you going?" Hunter asked Xavier.

"You didn't think I came all this way to watch you walk out into a storm and possibly never come back, did you?"

Hunter reached over, and the men slapped hands then pulled each other in. Without another word, they left the jet and stepped out into harsh winds and rain. Like men on a mission, they trekked to a small station that housed the hangars. Hunter pulled back on the door, but it was locked. With a strong fist, he beat against the door's frame. There was no movement inside, so Hunter knocked again. He looked over at Xavier then over to a BMW parked in the empty lot.

"It'll take us three hours to walk on a normal day. On this day, about five." Xavier mentioned.

Hunter cursed then rammed his fist against the door again. In five hours who knows what could have happened to Camilla. His stomach churned, and his gut tightened as he thought of losing her to the storm. With no other options in sight, Hunter slapped Xavier's shoulder with a backhand.

"Come on!" He said, infuriated.

The wind continued to whip around them, and the wetness from the blizzard would make their clothes feel like weights the longer they journeyed on foot.

"Hello!" A voice yelled behind them.

Hunter and Xavier turned around sharply, and relief flooded them both at the sight of the man standing at the door. They trudged back, and the Asian man allowed them entry.

"Do you have a car?" Hunter said as water dripped from him.

"You can't drive. It's too dangerous. I have a shelter in the back."

"Listen to me," Hunter said. "I'll pay you triple whatever your BMW is worth if you just give me the keys right now."

The man's eyes lurched. "What, do you have a death wish?"

"If that's what it takes," he said.

CAMILLA SAT on a barrel inside her parents' underground

shelter. The storm had seemed to go on forever, and sleep had evaded her while everyone else was knocked out in dreamland. The thunder and tussling of wind didn't seem so bad at first until a loud popping sound made her think the house was falling over. The foundation it sat on shook, and the walls groaned within. Camilla's tension mounted, and a crash could be heard above. Her thoughts stirred, and she wondered if it was the mirror that hung on the living room wall, but Camilla didn't have much time to dwell on it when the house shook again, and another dragging groan edged through the floorboards.

"The storm is going to uproot us at any minute," she said to only herself. Camilla bit down on her jaw and shut her eyes tight, but she couldn't sit still. Camilla needed motion to help shake off her fear. She moved from the barrel to pace the floor. Trying to take her mind off Hurricane Jasper, she removed the stick from her back pocket. Looking down at it, Camilla released a huge breath, and her mind pitched in a storm of its own. She put it back in her pocket then returned to the barrel, hoping and praying to God they would make it out of this alive.

Another loud crackling sounded throughout the house, like lightning spinning from the sky. It roused Camilla and the others. In a chair, Bernard glanced around then released a long breath.

"Is everyone okay?" He asked, his voice strained with anxiety.

Sharon stretched, and she and Corinne responded in unison, "We're okay."

Bernard stood and walked over to Camilla. "And how about you?"

Camilla eyed the gray hairs on her daddy's head and in his mustache and beard. She smiled softly. "I'm alive," she said. "Nervous, but still alive."

Bernard nodded. "I thought it was over for a minute. It had gotten so quiet."

"Yeah, me, too."

Bernard paused for a long while before speaking again. "Do you want to talk about it?" he said, referencing the pregnancy test she'd held when she ran through his front door.

Camilla swallowed just as a loud bang from the basement's door rapped in succession.

"Oh my God!" Camilla said, and they all rose to their feet.

It sounded like the door would rip off at any moment.

"Come over here!" Bernard said, gathering his family. "Stay in this corner, no matter what." The women huddled in the corner of the room, and Bernard walked toward the door.

"What are you doing?" Sharon asked.

"I'm checking things out, stay put."

"Bernard!"

Bernard kept walking.

"Daddy!" Camilla shouted.

But he wouldn't listen. In a desperate flee, Camilla ran across the room and grabbed Bernard's arm just as the door was ripped open. Bernard covered Camilla as her mother and Corinne screamed. After seconds of no strong wind hauling them away, both Bernard and Camilla slowly glanced upward.

Staring down at them with the will of a determined man, Hunter Valentine abided breathing like he had run a marathon. His broad shoulders rose and fell, and quickly, he dropped to his knees and held a hand out to help them.

"Hunter!?" Camilla screeched. "What— what're— are you crazy!?"

Camilla reached for his hand, and he hauled her out of the shelter into his arms. "Hell yeah, I'm crazy. Crazy about you."

Camilla's eyes widened, and she covered her mouth in a gasp. She had so many questions, but none of them seemed relevant right now. While she and Hunter stared each other down, Xavier helped pull the others from the basement.

"The storm has moved west," Hunter said. "What's left in its wake is the thunder I'm sure you heard. He saw the lingering questions in her eyes, but Camilla was so speechless that they stayed lodged in her throat. "I couldn't stay away knowing you were here. I love you too much, and I need you to marry me." A tear fell from Hunter's eyes. "You said you'd have my babies," he added, and Camilla laughed with tears of her own falling from her eyes.

"You're a fool!" She said. "You could've been killed!" She pounded his chest once with a closed fist.

"I don't care. It's not my death that I fear; it's yours."

Camilla's chest rocked as she cried harder in his arms. The two held each other, and Hunter pressed hot kisses against her face, neck and lips. He removed the princess cut diamond. It wasn't in a box or in some fashionable display.

It just sat on the tip of his fingers, casting a sharp bling that sparkled like the sun.

"Oh my God, you're serious!"

"I would never play with a situation such as this. Tell me," he said. "Please."

Astonished, Camilla cried harder, and she nodded frantically. "Yes, I'll marry you!"

Hunter pulled her in for a kiss, but Camilla stopped him with a hand to his chest. "There's something else."

"Okay…"

Camilla blushed then dropped her face, and Hunter lifted it back to his smoldering stare.

"Tell me."

Camilla opened her mouth to speak, then hesitated. "I'm… pregnant."

A flurry of chills encompassed them both, and Hunter's eyes lurched as everyone around them gasped. Camilla removed the test from her pocket and handed it over to Hunter.

Hunter glanced down at it but didn't reach for it not wanting to let Camilla go. More tears ran from his eyes, and he sank his mouth into hers, completely taking her breath away.

"I love you so fucking much," he said.

"I love you, too," she answered with streaming tears.

"Can we get out of here?"

"Yeah."

Although they both said it, neither of them made a move. Instead, Hunter kept her pinned to him as they were raptured in the heat of another pulse-stinging kiss.

THE END

DID you enjoy *No Holds Barred?* Subscribe to my <u>newsletter</u> or join my <u>Facebook Group</u> to get updates from me, the author! You can also pre-order the next installment featuring Xavier Valentine and Corinne Thomas: *A Risqué Engagement.*

<u>Connect with Me on Facebook!</u>
<u>Connect with Me on Instagram!</u>

Note from the Author

Thank you so much for reading *No Holds Barred,* In the Heart of a Valentine, book one. I hope you enjoyed Hunter and Camilla's story! Reviews are the lifeblood of independent writers. The more reviews we get, the more Amazon and others promote the book. If you want to see more books by me, Stephanie Nicole Norris, a review would let me know that you're enjoying the series. If you liked the book, I ask you to write a review on <u>Amazon.com,</u> Goodreads or wherever you go for your book information. Thank you so much. Doing so means a lot to me.

XOXO - <u>Stephanie</u>

Catch me at Atlanta Kickback 2018! With me will be my Falling for a Rose and In the Heart of a Valentine series!

Other Books by Stephanie Nicole Norris

Contemporary Romance

- Everything I Always Wanted (A Friends to Lovers Romance)
- Safe with Me (Falling for a Rose Book One)
- Enough (Falling for a Rose Book Two)
- Only If You Dare (Falling for a Rose Book Three)
- Fever (Falling for a Rose Book Four)
- A Lifetime with You (Falling for a Rose Book Five)
- She said Yes (Falling for a Rose Holiday Edition Book Six)
- Mine (Falling for a Rose Book Seven)
- The Sweetest Surrender (Falling for a Rose Book Eight)

Romantic Suspense Thrillers

- Beautiful Assassin
- Beautiful Assassin 2 Revelations
- Mistaken Identity
- Trouble in Paradise
- Vengeful Intentions (Trouble in Paradise 2)

- For Better and Worse (Trouble in Paradise 3)
- Until My Last Breath (Trouble in Paradise 4)

Christian Romantic Suspense

- Broken
- Reckless Reloaded

Crime Fiction

- Prowl
- Prowl 2
- Hidden

Fantasy

- Golden (Rapunzel's F'd Up Fairytale)

Non-Fiction

- Against All Odds (Surviving the Neonatal Intensive Care Unit) *Non-Fiction

About the Author

Stephanie Nicole Norris is an author from Chattanooga, Tennessee, with a humble beginning. She was raised with six siblings by her mother Jessica Ward. Always being a lover of reading, during Stephanie's teenage years, her joy was running to the bookmobile to read stories by R. L. Stine.

After becoming a young adult, her love for romance sparked, leaving her captivated by heroes and heroines alike. With a big imagination and a creative heart, Stephanie penned her first novel *Trouble in Paradise* and self-published it in 2012. Her debut novel turned into a four-book series packed with romance, drama, and suspense. As a prolific writer, Stephanie's catalog continues to grow. Her books can be found on her website and Amazon. Stephanie is inspired by the likes of Donna Hill, Eric Jerome Dickey, Jackie Collins, and more. She currently resides in Tennessee with her husband and two-year-old son.

https://stephanienicolenorris.com/

Made in the USA
Lexington, KY
16 June 2018